The Perfect Blindside

The Perfect BLINDSIDE

By Leslea Wahl

Pauline
BOOKS & MEDIA
Boston

Library of Congress Cataloging-in-Publication Data

Wahl, Leslea.
The perfect blindside / by Leslea Wahl.
pages cm
Summary: Told in their separate voices, Jake, an Olympic snowboarder
whose fame has gone to his head, and Sophie, a high school junior and
big fan of Jake's, connect at high school and soon find themselves
working together to uncover who has framed him for drug possession and
other misdeeds.
ISBN 978–0–8198–6013–2—ISBN 0–8198–6013–1 (pbk.)
[1. Snowboarding—Fiction. 2. Olympic athletes—Fiction. 3. Celebrities—
Fiction. 4. Conduct of life—Fiction. 5. Christian life—Fiction. 6. Crime and
criminals—Fiction.] I. Title.
PZ7.1.W35Per 2015
[Fic]—dc23
                                         2014037909

Cover and interior design by Mary Joseph Peterson, FSP

Cover photo by iStockPhoto/aurumarcus

Published by Pauline Books & Media, 50 Saint Pauls Avenue, Boston, MA
02130–3491

Printed in the U.S.A.

www.pauline.org

Pauline Books & Media is the publishing house of the Daughters of St.
Paul, an international congregation of women religious serving the Church
with the communications media.

1 2 3 4 5 6 7 8 9   19 18 17 16 15

To my husband for his unconditional support,
my children who inspire me daily,
and to God for leading me
on this amazing journey.

Contents

Chapter 1

Jake

I have a theory. Every person I've ever met in the past year fits into one of three categories. They're either Walkers, Talkers, or Stalkers.

Walkers are those who stare from a distance, completely lacking the guts to approach me, then slowly walk away pretending they don't care.

Talkers include my parents, coach, and advisors. They have this obsessive need to always tell me what to do.

Stalkers are the most common, and they all want something. It could be an old lady at the grocery store wanting an autograph for her grandkids. It could be little kids making a scene in the middle of a restaurant when they recognize me. It could be an executive wanting me to sell hair gel . . . or jeans . . . or whatever. Or it could be a girl at the mall, who slips me her phone number. (Okay, that one I actually like.)

I get it. I'm Jake Taylor. Snowboarding phenom. But sometimes a guy just wants to eat his burger in peace, away from the autograph seekers and camera flashes.

Journalists are by far the most annoying group. They're usually a combination of all three: Stalkers because they need me; Walkers since they try to act indifferent when meeting me; and Talkers because they always finish with a piece of useless advice.

And can their stupid interviews be any more annoying? To think I used to be excited about them. Hard to believe they get paid to ask dumb questions. Sure, I have a cool story, but do you have any idea how mind-numbing it is to repeat it 150 times?

It never fails. The reporters have this obsessive need to ask what it feels like to ride the halfpipe. At first I would try to explain the rush of wind and adrenaline as I soar up the twenty-two foot wall, how my board keeps rising, and for a moment everything stops and I'm flying. Pulling my rotation high above the lip, gravity does its thing and I hurtle back toward the edge in a freefall. I hang on to the landing, then rocket up the other side with even more momentum and speed, anticipating the next trick. It's a mix of feeling totally in control one second and completely out of control the next. My coach calls it physics in motion. I call it awesome.

But after answering the same questions endless times, I got bored with my explanation. So the last time a reporter wanted to know how it felt, I answered, "The mix of fear, adrenaline, and excitement make an addictive high." Unfortunately my agent got on my case because I said "addictive high." "Jake, those words don't portray the sparkly clean image we're going for."

Whatever.

Then there are stupid questions, like, "How does it feel to be the Olympic Silver Medalist?"

Seriously? How do you think it feels? Freakin' amazing.

Or, how about the original, "Tell us about your Olympic experience." I stick with the polite, "It was incredible," mostly because I don't know how else to answer. I've spent a lot of time trying to remember that week, but I can't. Training runs, marching in the Opening Ceremony, hanging out at the Olympic Village—it all runs together.

Six months of insane frenzy later, I'm in a new town ready to start the first day of my junior year of high school. Thrilling. Not. After traveling around the world and hanging out with celebrities, sitting in a classroom with a bunch of nobody kids is pointless.

I'd rather ditch the whole school thing and get a private tutor like other athletes and actors. I mean, they are the kind of people I should be hanging out with anyway. But no. My parents want me to have "the high school experience." Just because they loved high school back in the day doesn't mean it fits my life.

Before I leave my bedroom, ready to get this day over with, I glance at my reflection, but barely recognize my now famous face. It's been such a whirlwind that sometimes I wonder who I really am.

The bare walls of the hallway and staircase lead me down toward the kitchen for breakfast. At the base of the steps, I pass the living room, still bulging with moving boxes. The stone fireplace with the near life-size portrait of me mid-air,

3

pulling a back-scratcher is the focal point of the room. That picture and my silver medal in its display case on the mantel are the only evidence of my sport. All the other stuff—trophies, awards, framed magazine covers—will soon line the walls of the new rec room in the basement. My own little shrine.

The scent of frying bacon steers me the rest of the way to the kitchen. My dad sits at his usual spot at the head of the table. He stabs the newspaper with his finger.

"Have you seen the headlines?" he asks, not bothering to wait for an answer. "Apparently there's a growing drug problem in resort towns around here. The authorities are trying to figure out where the supply is coming from, but so far they haven't had any leads."

"Just one more reason to live here in Silver Springs, away from all the problems of the touristy areas," Mom says as she works at the stove.

"Oh, don't be fooled by this place," I warn them as I sit down at the table. "There's plenty of crime here. Do you know there's a huge cruising problem along that one block of Main Street? Someone actually got up to thirty miles an hour. And rumor has it there's a gang in town. A cow tipping gang. Maybe we should move to a cave to protect me from the evils of this place."

"There aren't any cows around here," counters Dad, ignoring my sarcasm. "That was back in Kansas. We're now in the Colorado Rockies."

"Maybe he means moose tipping," Mom helpfully adds as she sets a huge mound of food in front of me.

"Technically, I don't think you can tip a moose," Dad says, between sips of coffee.

I stare at them. After a summer of constant togetherness, maybe school, no matter how lame it is, would be better than this. "You guys are hilarious."

"Jake, you've got to admit, Silver Springs looks exactly like those towns in the old westerns we used to watch."

"Dad, that was when I was six. Now I'm sixteen and don't want to live in an old mining town with no friends. Not cool."

"Hey, I remember you were as excited about moving to Colorado as we were," says Mom.

"Yeah, that's when I thought we would move to Vail and be near my teammates. Who knew you'd choose the most boring town in existence?"

"We've talked about this. Silver Springs is the perfect location, fairly close to your training area and not far from Denver and the airport."

I dig into my breakfast and do my best to ignore them as my dad's attention turns back to the newspaper.

I hate not being on my own yet. My parents and I have argued about school and this no-where town all summer, ever since they freaked about my fame and went all "family-values" on me. I'm sick of them running my life.

Rachael, my snowboarding teammate, tired of my complaints, told me to ride it out and keep the peace at home. She pointed out that fighting won't change their minds and will only make the wait to be on my own seem longer. I don't know if it'll work, but I'm giving it a try. I mean . . . Rachael's cool . . . she's like the big sister I don't have. So my plan is to serve out my sentence at home and train with the team as much as possible. But as soon as I graduate, I'm outta here.

"Hey," Dad says, interrupting my thoughts. "There's something here in the Editorial section about an incident that happened a few months ago up at the mine. It says two hikers were wandering through the mine when they claim they were chased out by a ghost. They were laughed out of town, but it sparked the retelling of a whole bunch of ghost stories."

"Sounds like those hikers took advantage of the rise in drugs here in the state," jokes Mom.

"Wait. Can we go back to the whole 'exploring the mine' thing? That's cool. You mean I can actually get into that place?" I ask.

"No. Absolutely not. There is no way you're going into a mine. You could be bitten by wild animals, get tetanus stepping on a rusty tool, become lost or trapped in a collapse. It's way too dangerous," Mom says and shivers thinking of all the dangerous possibilities. As if snowboarding doesn't have any of those.

Right. The one semi-interesting thing in this town, and she forbids me to check it out. I don't think so. I reach for my car keys on the counter where I tossed them yesterday, but Mom grabs my arm.

"Oh Jake, we're taking your jeep in today to get snow tires. The ones it came with may look good, but you don't want to drive with them when it starts snowing. I'll take you to school today." She smiles at me like this is good news.

"Perfect. The epitome of coolness—being driven to my new school by my mommy."

"At least it's not a minivan," pipes in Dad.

Climbing into the SUV, I wonder if this day could get any more annoying.

"Jake," Mom says as she steers down our long driveway, "I've been thinking. Do you want to invite Rick and Jon to visit sometime?"

Yep . . . more annoying.

"We'll see," I answer, turning my head so she can't see my scowl.

"It must be hard to be away from them. Maybe they can come out over fall break."

"I'm sure they're busy."

"You three were constantly together ever since kindergarten . . . climbing trees or catching frogs or something. You must miss them. And I'm sure they miss you too."

I glare out the window, clenching my fist as we pass through town toward the high school. Rick and Jon. My so-called best friends. The memory of them purposely ignoring me still burns. In three short months they went from being my constant companions to refusing to return my phone calls. The most exciting time of my life was also the loneliest. I mean, it completely bites having something so incredible happen and no friends to share it with. Nope. Don't really miss them. It's mutual.

"Jake, give this place a chance," my mom continues. "You'll have friends here before you know it."

"Mom, I know the drill. Anyone new is automatically the focus of attention. Even if I wasn't already a household name, I'd be the topic of gossip."

Although I've gotten used to having all eyes on me, constantly being watched gets old. It would be nice to have someone to chill with, I just doubt that can happen here—or anywhere.

As we round the last bend my mom gives me one last piece of motherly advice.

"Jake, just try to fit in." Then she gasps, "Oh, no."

My head snaps forward and I groan. So much for trying to fit in.

Chapter 2

Sophie

"Take me out to the ball game. Take me out with the crowd . . ."

Uhh . . . what? I slap at the alarm.

The tune continues. Not the alarm.

Through squinted eyes I search the grey shadows of my bedroom. The music seems to be coming from my desk.

Sam.

Note to self: *Kill him later.*

Ten-year-old little brothers and cell phones don't mix. Sam's always messing with my settings. Ringtones are apparently his newest discovery. At least I was spared the total humiliation of anyone from school hearing it.

Before the singer begins to call the strikes, I stumble out of bed and lunge toward my desk, but manage to slam my toe into the chair. Grimacing, I yank my phone from its charger. As I answer it with one hand, I grab my throbbing toe with the other and hop back to bed.

"What?" I grunt as I flop onto my mattress.

"Sophie?" chirps my best friend.

"Kate . . . I was asleep. What do you want?" I don't know why I ask. I already know what she's calling about.

"What are you going to wear today?"

It's too early for this again. "I already told you five times yesterday, *I . . . don't . . . know.*"

"Come on, it's the first day of school. We're finally juniors. We've been looking forward to this for like—forever! How can you not be excited? Today's our chance to meet *him*." She finally stops for a breath.

"Joy," I mutter.

"Soph, you're being irrational."

"Irrational? What are you, a shrink?"

"Hey, don't change the subject. This is going to be the best year ever. Come on, you're usually as excited as I am. Don't you remember in fifth grade when we met early before school so we could braid each other's hair?"

"I remember," I say, pulling the phone further from my ear. Her bubbliness is too much to take.

"What about seventh grade, when we did extra chores and earned enough money to buy matching outfits?"

"We looked like dorks."

"And then before ninth grade, when we stayed up all night texting each other?"

"I fell asleep in class."

"Come on, Grumpy, I know your inner excitement is hiding in there somewhere." She sounds like she's about to burst into a cheer at any moment.

"What's the purpose of this trip down memory lane?"

"To help you remember you love going back to school."

She's right, which I hate to admit. The first day of school is usually one of my favorite days of the year. Not today though. This one is going to be very different. This one I'm dreading.

"So, what are you going to wear?" she probes, her decibel level increasing. "We need to look *good* when we finally meet him. First impressions—"

"Good-bye, Kate," I interrupt as I hang up grumbling.

Falling back asleep is probably impossible now, but I'm determined to try. I burrow deep beneath my covers, hoping to avoid the dread of this day.

What do I care what "he" thinks of me? He's an arrogant jerk. And because of him I'm completely broke, spent a week of my summer break grounded, and nearly lost my precious car.

I ponder how my opinion of him has changed over the last few months. Eight months ago I had never even heard of Jake Taylor. No one had. Then came the Winter Olympics. Amazing how such an awesome international event could end up ruining my junior year of high school.

Like the rest of the country, I was spellbound watching him during the Olympics. I mean, here was this sixteen-year-old snowboarder from Kansas, of all places, who wasn't even supposed to be there. But a freak set of circumstances landed him on the team. With each run he took, his tricks got bigger and more insane. Then he shocked everyone and won the silver medal. His unlikely story and stellar good looks made him an instant celebrity. Jake Taylor's handsome face soon graced every magazine and TV talk show.

Like every other teenage girl I was completely fascinated by the guy. I'm not proud to admit that I snatched my dad's sports magazine in order to stare at the full-page spread about him. His striking blue eyes peering out from under that dark hair were too irresistible. And something about his mischievous grin and dimples made me watch as many of his interviews as possible.

Then on a Monday morning in June the news broke and spread through town like an irritating rash. Actually, at that point I was beyond excited when I heard it. Jake Taylor and his family were moving to Silver Springs!

Soon after he and his parents arrived, Kate and I caught a glimpse of him walking down Main Street. He looked like a model with his lean body in worn jeans, white T-shirt, and designer shades. With his dark hair—cut short on the sides and back, longer in the front—framing that cute face. I thought I'd died and gone to heaven. But then Mr. Wonderful started to show his true colors and fell off his pedestal.

Who am I kidding? Sleep is not happening. I'm wide awake and completely annoyed, and not because of Kate's unwelcome wake-up call. After throwing the covers off, I hobble, careful of my sore toe, to the bathroom. Catching my reflection in the mirror—mismatched pajamas and brown rat's nest, otherwise known as my hair—does nothing to improve my mood.

Irrational? I can't believe Kate thinks *I'm* irrational. I'm the only rational one around. The "A" I got in English last year, when we discussed truth in advertising and the importance of image in the media, paid off. I seem to be the only one who sees past Jake Taylor's carefully-crafted image and has figured out that Mr. Boy-Next-Door isn't what he appears to be.

I admit I should have figured it out sooner. The real boy next door looks like Ray Harlin, with greasy hair and stubby fingers. He doesn't have the kind of smile that compels you to spend ridiculous amounts of time obsessing over his fan page. The real boy next door doesn't have mesmerizing blue eyes that make you daydream during science and miss an assignment, thus ruining your perfect grade.

And now the first day of school will be ruined because of him. Everyone will fawn all over him, and he doesn't deserve it. Seriously, why did Jake Taylor and his family have to come to Silver Springs? Of all the other towns they could have chosen, why did they have to move here?

People say, "Good things come to those who wait," but I'm having a hard time believing it. I go to Mass every weekend, volunteer at Vacation Bible School, and have attended Sunday school all these years. And this is my reward?

Life is so unfair. *Lord, I know you're really great at performing miracles, so if you could somehow miraculously make this year not totally the worst ever—that would be amazing.*

After a quick shower, I rummage through my closet in search of something to wear. As I tromp downstairs for breakfast, I try to convince myself things will be fine. Sure, everyone will follow Jake around for a while, but seriously, how long can that last? He'll probably be away waxing his board—or whatever jocks do—most of the time. Besides, I doubt he'll be in any of my classes. It'll be easy to avoid him.

No chance we'll be hanging out with the same people. My friends all use complete sentences—usually.

"Morning, Sunshine," Mom greets as I enter the kitchen.

"Morning."

"Are you excited about today? I can't believe you're a junior."

"Yeah."

"It seems like yesterday you were all dressed up in your cute little Mary Jane's, ready for your first day of kindergarten."

"Extremely stylish."

"And now you're a junior driving yourself to school," she sighs. "Are you excited about showing off your new car?"

"*That* I'm looking forward to."

"Oh, Mrs. Meyers called this morning. Duchess is missing again. That dog is quite a handful. Can you keep an eye out for her?"

"I'll watch for her, but she'll probably go home for dinner like last time."

"Have a wonderful first day of school, sweetheart."

Not likely, but I suppose with God anything is possible. I grab my keys, camera (never want to leave home without it), and a granola bar, then trudge out the door.

Dear Jesus, help everything to be normal today. Please don't let Jake Taylor's presence change everything.

While I cautiously drive through town and make my way to school, I smile picturing everyone's face as I pull into the parking lot in my beautiful little bug. Since lots of the students at Silver Springs High come from neighboring towns, they haven't seen my new wheels. I picture the surprise and envy on their faces when they see my car for the first time. My grin widens. It'll be awesome. I'm sure Mallory will show up in some sports car, and her flock of followers will drool over her as usual. But, for now, this is my fantasy, and all eyes are on my cute green car and, of course, on me.

The high school is located on the town's far side, which, let's face it, is a relative term since nothing in this town is far. Because the building is "new" and big and doesn't fit in with our whole turn-of-the-century-mining-town look, it was built at the edge of Silver Springs. The place is in constant use though. Everything from basketball tournaments to Bingo nights is held in the gym.

When I round the last bend, the sight that greets me causes my heart to plummet and my smile to vanish. I knew I was right. *Everything* has changed. There will be no catching up with friends in the hallways before class. There will be no gossiping in the cafeteria at lunch time. There will be no one checking out my new wheels. Nope, everyone is focused on one person.

The media frenzy is insane. Three vans from rival Denver news stations have taken over the place. Their cameras and lights are set up. Perfect-looking reporters interview eager students. Cars line both sides of the road. Journalists swarm everywhere, while townspeople of all ages gather in groups near the school.

Welcome to life with Jake Taylor.

I slowly edge around the commotion, trying not to run over anyone. Eventually I find an open spot at the far end of the parking lot. I inch into the tiny space between a rusty old truck and a delivery van. So help me, if my new car's door gets dinged because of Mr. Testosterone . . . I *will* hand deliver the repair bill to him.

Carefully, I open my door, then wiggle out of the car. I yank my backpack out in a huff. I had planned on taking some photos to commemorate the first day back at school but decide I have no desire to capture this madness, so I leave the camera and slam the car door shut in protest. Kate is a few yards ahead and I hurry to catch up with her. She, of course, looks fantastic in her cute capris and layered tops but she kind of overdid the make-up.

"Hey, Kate."

"Sophie! Isn't this exciting? We might be on the news tonight. Have you seen Jake yet this morning?" she asks, tucking strands of her blonde bob behind her ears.

"No, I haven't had the privilege." Geesh.

Kate stops in her tracks to examine me; her eyes narrow. "That's what you chose to wear on the most exciting day ever? Old jeans and a hoodie?"

"They're my favorites. Besides, I don't have anything new to wear since I used all my babysitting money to pay the higher car insurance, thanks to Mr. Perfect."

"Soph, that first ticket you got wasn't really his fault."

"Well, if *he* weren't in town I wouldn't have been speeding to your house so we could catch a glimpse of him, right? And the second ticket was totally his fault. He tailgated me!"

"Well . . . sometimes you do drive like my grandma."

"Hey, I wasn't about to risk getting another speeding ticket. My parents made it clear—one more and I can kiss my driving privileges good-bye till I'm as old as your grandma. Besides, he was being a jerk, riding my bumper. I thought he was going to hit me. He made me so nervous I totally missed the stop sign and blew right past it."

"And as Deputy Grady pulled you over," she continues in a sing-song voice, "Mr. Renegade flew past with a wave. I know, you've told me a *million* times."

"Don't forget that when I finally made it to town I had to park two blocks away because Jake the Jerk had the nerve to take two parking spots on Main Street for his precious jeep. I ruined my new white sneakers trudging through the mud!"

"Sophie, you're making way too big a deal about this."

"You know that's not the *only* reason I think he's a creep."

"You haven't even met him yet. Seriously, Soph, give him a chance!"

"I don't need to meet him to know what he's like."

Just then the chaos around the school goes extreme. The cameras flash, the crowd roars, and the drumline bangs out some annoyingly peppy rhythm. A shiny black SUV pulls up to the front entrance and stops directly beneath a giant banner that reads, "Welcome Jake Taylor." Wow. Clever. I wonder how long it took them to come up with that. The excitement level spikes, and the squealing of dozens of girls gives me a headache.

Mr. Wonderful has arrived.

He steps out of the SUV, gives a quick wave and smile to his adoring fans, then dodges into the school. If reporters wanted a statement, I guess they're disappointed. Can anyone tell me why this is even remotely newsworthy?

Ten minutes later, I'm standing in front of my new locker, my silver home away from home. Queen Bee Mallory Shepherd and her flock of wanna-bees push their way through the narrow hallway, like they own the place.

To make the day even more perfect, Mallory has the locker directly across the hall from mine. Of course she does. I'll be blessed with her presence, several times a day. All year long. *Lord, what did I do to deserve this?* Mallory dramatically shuts her locker and whirls around in a cloud of perfume, which makes my headache even worse. She then struts down the hall with her spineless posse in tow.

I dump my things in my locker, not sure I'll be able to remember the new combination any time soon. Pushing my way through the crowd, I sulk off to my first subject of the day—Pre-Calc—which, of course, is at the opposite end of the school.

The first few classes go along as expected. Usual first day stuff except for the irritating non-stop talk about Jake.

Walking into Honors English, I check out the familiar faces. All the usual suspects are present. I search the rows for an open seat, then freeze in shock. Sitting at the back of the class is Jake Taylor. My eyes betray me and scan him from head to toe. He's wearing jeans and a blue polo shirt that matches his eyes perfectly. A white T-shirt peaks out from the unbuttoned collar. He's beautiful. Too bad he's such a jerk.

My cheeks start to burn as I realize he's caught me staring at him. Why is he watching me? Slowly I check over my shoulder, hoping there's something behind me that has captured his attention. Nope. He's looking at me.

Anxious to stop the awkward moment, I slide into an empty seat. Now I'm sitting in the front of the class like one of the nerds. Perfect. Just perfect.

What is he doing here anyway? I didn't expect to find him in any of my honors classes, him being a jock and all. I know I'm stereotyping, but seriously, who would have thought it?

By the time lunch finally arrives, I'm famished. Once in the bright cafeteria, my eyes immediately go to our table to see if Kate has arrived yet. And, of course, sitting at said table like he owns the place is Mr. Jake Taylor. Are you kidding me? Of all the tables in the lunchroom, he had to choose the one Kate and I have been sitting at with our friends for the past two years? Who does he think he is, rolling—or in his case snowboarding—into town and taking over everything?

Grudgingly, I join the lunch line and grab some food, although I've lost my appetite. Kate, at a table in the far corner, wildly waves her arms to get my attention. I nod and start the long trek over to her, my sneakers squeaking on the linoleum floor. The sound is truly cringeworthy—unusually loud . . . irritatingly loud. Where is all the normal cafeteria noise? The place is unsettlingly quiet. Totally embarrassed at the scene I'm making, I try to nonchalantly tiptoe across the room. Then it dawns on me—no one is paying attention to me or my squeaky shoes. Everyone is locked in a hypnotic trance, watching Jake eat. Oh brother!

"He's cuter than usual today," whispers Kate when at last I reach the table.

"I hadn't noticed." I plop my tray on the table.

"I wish I had enough nerve to talk to him, but I don't know what I'd say." Kate stares dreamily at him.

"How about, 'Go away'?" I grumble as I stab a piece of chicken with my fork.

"Sophie, you're being impossible. Remember all those times we wished something exciting would happen around here? Well, it finally has."

I glance over at "his" table and watch a few brave kids approach him.

Small towns are awesome—when you're young. You can run around all day with no worries, everyone watching out for each other. But as you get older those same small towns become rather mundane. Kate and I have spent hours day-dreaming of adventures that could make this place interesting. Heck, I've even prayed for excitement. Granted, it may not have been the most unselfish prayer ever, and I can imagine what Father Scott would say, but it's what I longed for. That's probably why Kate and I and everyone else at this high school voraciously watched the Olympics last winter. It was an escape from our completely boring lives. How pathetic is it when TV is the highlight of your day?

Kate's right. Something new has happened, and he's changed Silver Springs. Turns out I'm not a big fan of change. *This* is not what I wanted, God!

"Soph? Hello Sophie . . . are you still with me?" asks Kate. "Give him a chance."

"Kate, if you watch him long enough, you'll eventually see what I see," I sigh.

"Oh, I'm watching him all right," she answers, still ogling him.

But too bad for her because Jake quickly gathers his stuff, dumps his tray, and then saunters out the door. Why can't anyone else see that he thinks he's too good for us?

The afternoon goes by without any more drama. No run-ins with Mallory. No more classes with Jake. When the final bell rings, Kate meets me at my locker and asks if I want to go get ice cream in town to celebrate our first day. I don't know about celebrating, but I'd never turn down an ice cream sundae.

On the drive to Main Street, Kate rambles on about her classes, the newest gossip she heard, and which guys have already made her new PB&J lists (Potential Boyfriends and Jerks).

"You know, it's never too soon to start scoping out the guys."

"Kate, there aren't many boys around here to get excited about. We've known them all since forever."

"Enough with the mood, Soph. Where's my fun-loving friend?" she pleads.

"Okay. Sorry. I'll try harder."

I pull into one of the angled parking spots near the old hitchin' post, where bikes instead of horses are now tied up. We climb the worn wooden steps to the boardwalk that runs along the front of the businesses. All the shops here on Main Street are in the original mining town buildings. The Cold Rush by far has the coolest location. We push our way through the swinging saloon doors that lead into the ice-cream parlor. The antique wooden bar stretches along the back wall. But instead of bottles of booze, glass jars filled with ice cream toppings line the front of the huge mirror.

We maneuver our way through the crowded shop. Apparently half the school had the same brilliant idea. After we order our hot fudge sundaes, we belly up to the bar at the far end of the room. I slide a spoonful of drippy gooeyness in my mouth. Ah, just what I needed.

"When do you think we should start working on the yearbook?" Kate asks.

"Soon. Most of the clubs and activities will start this week." We love being on the yearbook committee—our way of checking out all the groups at school. We used to contribute to the school newspaper, but it's produced entirely in the journalism elective class, which is full of annoying freshmen, so now we just focus on the yearbook.

"The football team has already started practice. Is your camera ready to go?" Kate's the writer, I'm the photographer. Truth be told, I wouldn't mind doing it all myself since I want to study photojournalism in college, but it's more fun work-ing together.

"Yeah, and with your stellar reporting skills our coverage of all the activities will be superb."

"Now that we're upper classmen we can practically run the whole thing by ourselves."

"We already have Mr. Henry wrapped around our fingers," I agree. The yearbook advisor is a fan of our work. The only senior on the yearbook staff prefers the behind-the-scenes jobs of copyeditor and layout supervisor. Works for us.

"Oh. My. Gosh," Kate blurts out, spoon midair, chocolate syrup dripping onto the bar. She does over dramatic well. "Check out the table in front of the window. I can't believe it."

Humoring her, I look around to locate whatever has her all worked up. Jake. With Mallory—of course—who tosses her head back in fake laughter, her long blonde hair cascading down her back. Then she leans in close and says something to him that makes him grin. Boy, didn't take her long. I must admit, they make a perfect pair. Both conceited and full of themselves.

"Come on, it's our chance to go say 'hi,'" states Kate.

"Are you crazy? I don't want to talk to him."

"You said you'd try," she coaxes.

"But he doesn't even want to live here; why should we bend over backward to make him feel welcome?"

"You're still upset by what he said in the newspaper?"

"I already explained this. He said all the right things, but it was *how* he said them."

"Oh, that makes perfect sense," says Kate as she rolls her eyes at me.

"Seriously, he said, 'It *seems* like a nice place to live.' I've read enough interviews to know Jake uses words like 'wicked' and 'stoked' when talking about things he's into. He didn't use them, so he obviously doesn't want to be here."

"Sophie, *we* don't want to be in Silver Springs, why should he?"

"If you weren't so busy wiping the drool off your chin when we saw him at the pizzeria, you would've seen his attitude there."

"He let that mother take his photo with her son."

"Yes, but after she asked him and turned around to get her camera, Jake totally rolled his eyes, then had the nerve to flash his perfect, fake smile for the photo. He's conceited. I mean, look who he's with. Mallory was the last new person to move to town and that hasn't worked out so great. Maybe we should stop wishing for new and exciting. Nothing good comes from it."

"Whatever." Kate slides off her stool and grabs my arm.

The girl has seriously lost her mind. I'd rather jab myself with a fork than go talk to them, but I can't stand to watch her crash and burn all alone so I let her drag me along.

"Excuse us," she says as we arrive at their table. Jake leans back in his chair, looking us up and down with an arrogant smirk.

"Yes? Would you like an autograph?" he asks while Mallory shoots me a smug look.

An autograph? He seriously thinks we walked over here to get an autograph? This guy is unbelievable. All those mid-air flips he does has knocked a few too many brain cells loose.

"No, we don't want your autograph," I spit out. Kate elbows me in the side before I get a chance to tell him where he can stick his autograph.

"I'm Kate and this is Sophie. We go to school with you and wanted to welcome you to Silver Springs. How are you enjoying it so far?"

"Oh. Well, it's . . . quaint," he answers. Mallory giggles.

Quaint? Are you kidding me? How dare he make fun of our town. Forget the fact Kate and I are constantly ragging on small town life. He hasn't been here long enough to earn the right to diss this place.

Kate continues to play nice while I give him one of my death ray looks, the kind that sends Sam running. But Jake keeps watching me with that stupid grin on his face, amused by my anger. This guy is infuriating. I finally give up, spin on my heel, and walk back to my melting ice cream.

Kate hurries after me. "I can't believe we actually talked to him!" she squeals.

"What?" How can she be completely oblivious to what a jerk this guy is?

I start to say something but decide it's not worth it. Besides, my headache has returned.

Chapter 3

Jake

"Hi, Jake. Mind if we join you?"

I look up from the strange brown blob which I assumed was chicken smothered in gravy but now am thinking is meatloaf. Mallory, her cheerleading uniform showing off her legs, and her pack of tag-alongs surround what, after one week, has become my table in the cafeteria. My own personal cheerleading squad . . . sweet. Their appearance interrupts my contemplation of whether or not to sample the gelatinous mass on my tray.

"Sure, ladies."

Mallory has been following me since Monday when she strutted up to my table at the Cold Rush and made herself comfortable. Hey, not complaining. Hanging out with a smokin' hot cheerleader isn't the worst thing in the world. She keeps hinting at us going out. But I'm not sure how involved I want to get. Integrating into Silver Springs doesn't fit in with my master plan of getting out of here as soon as possible.

Tommy would say I'm an idiot for not taking advantage of all this interest from the opposite sex. Which I'm pretty sure is his favorite part of snowboarding superstardom. His reputation of being a master at having one, two, or more of the hottest girls on his arms wherever he goes is legendary. But that's not my style.

Actually, all this attention from the female persuasion is new to me. I went from dorky middle schooler, more interested in video games and skateboards, to nonstop training and no time for girls. Then fame hit and they started to swarm. I'd never admit it to Tommy, but it's all a bit overwhelming. I guess I'm not cut out to be a "player."

"How has your first week been?" Mallory asks, sliding in right next to me.

"Pretty good. I haven't gotten lost yet."

The gaggle giggles.

Finally, week one will soon be over. Thankfully things have calmed down a little. Most people have gotten bored with staring at me during lunch, which is good because eating spaghetti with a room full of people who watch your every move would make anyone self-conscious. And I haven't noticed the cell phone paparazzi lurking in the hallways since Wednesday. So, all in all, I guess week one was a success.

Following Mallory's lead, her friends start to talk.

"I loved watching you in the Olympics."

"I still remember your last run, the whole team came out and tackled you."

"Yeah, champagne was sprayed everywhere. What'd that feel like?"

"Sticky," I answer.

More giggles.

Not going to tell them that it actually felt like being on a merry-go-round, not being able to focus on anything around you.

"Everyone was so excited. Mr. Gibbs even taped the medal ceremony. We all watched it the next day in Civics class," says Mallory.

I can't help but frown, thinking about the ceremony. Tommy and I stood next to each other in front of a huge crowd. First the German's name was announced, then mine. I know I stepped forward, was handed flowers, and the silver medal was placed around my neck. I know Tommy received his gold medal and the Star Spangled Banner played as our flags were raised. I know all this because I've seen the replay, but my own memory is a blur.

"What do you do with your free time? Any hobbies?" asks one of the girls, pulling me back into the conversation.

I look at the eager eyes of my inquisitors. Free time? I can't even remember the last time I just hung out.

"Tell me, what do you all do around here for fun?" I ask, changing the subject.

"Well, tonight's an away football game. We're all going. You should come, too."

"Maybe another time," I answer. I have no desire to spend any more time than necessary with these people.

"There's not much to do in this pathetic town," Mallory adds, stating the obvious.

"You can always go down to Denver for some excitement, and we could go with you."

"Homecoming is next month. And afterward there's a dance."

"And of course there's the Snow Ball."

"The what?" I ask.

Several of the girls open their mouths to explain but Mallory takes charge, silencing them all with a look. "The Snow Ball is a ridiculous tradition this whole town loves. The first time it snows at least six inches, the town gets all excited and has a dance here at the school gym." She finishes with a dramatic roll of her eyes.

My attention shifts then as the only other girl besides Mallory to catch my eye this week walks by the table. She's totally different from every girl I've met since winning silver. She's beautiful, but instead of smiling and flirting or laughing at everything I say, she glares at me with icy green eyes. Antagonizing her has become my new pastime. Every time I pass her in the hall or see her in class, I make an extra effort to give her a smile or head nod. Her cold, withering looks would make a lesser man scared.

When she glances at me, lunch tray clutched in her hands, I wink at her. She responds with her usual scowl, then turns away with a flip of her wavy brown hair.

"Hey, who's the Ice Princess?" I ask the cheerleaders.

"Oh, that's Sophie Metcalf."

"Her dad's a doctor, and her mom's the town librarian."

"She's a brainiac, always stressed about her GPA."

"I'd rather hear about some of the famous people you've met." Mallory bluntly changes the subject.

Lucky for me, the bell rings and saves me. "Well, see you later," I say as I take my brown blob and dump it in the trash.

Somehow I make it through the rest of the day without falling asleep. Staying awake when you don't care at all about what the teacher's saying is quite hard. After my last class, I book it out to the parking lot before Mallory can find me. I've had enough for one week and just want to get out of here. As I near the jeep some dude skateboards toward me. His laid-back surfer vibe seems out of place in Colorado.

As he approaches, he flips his long brown bangs out of his eyes. "Hey."

"Hey. Nice board," I say, admiring his gear.

"Thanks. You shred?" He stops and flips his board up, grabbing it in his hand.

"Yeah, I started on a skateboard."

"Ever meet Hawk?"

"This summer at a charity event." Meeting Tony Hawk was one of the coolest perks of the year.

"Dude. Want to ride with us sometime?"

Despite my resolve not to immerse myself in this town, the thought of riding with some fellow skateboarders is too appealing.

"Cool. I'm Jake."

"Yeah, I know. I'm Chad."

After a fist bump, he drops his board and rides off toward some other guys near the school. They look back at me and I give them a nod.

Geez, I didn't even realize how much I missed the wind whipping past my face, the whir of the wheels on the pavement, the jumping off curbs and flipping of the board. But mostly I miss the ribbing and lighthearted trash-talking with friends.

Climbing in the jeep, I crank the tunes and throw it in reverse. Got to get out of here before I'm trapped behind the slow drivers. I can't stand the ones that won't at least go the speed limit. I zip through town, and by the time I pull into the circle drive in front of my house, all thoughts of school have vanished.

"How was your day, Jake?" Mom asks as I walk through the back door. The tantalizing smell of her baking fills the kitchen.

"Fine," I answer, not in the mood to talk. "I'm going for a run." It's one of the things I actually like about living here: running, even in the high altitude. No suffocating humid air like in Kansas. Maybe I'll try to find the mine. I've got nothing else to do.

Taking the steps two at a time, I head upstairs to change. When I enter my room I see Mom's been doing more than just baking today. My posters and collection of baseball pennants now hang on the walls. The souvenirs from our family vacations have been carefully placed on the shelves above my desk. She's been hassling me for weeks to unpack, but so far I haven't been motivated. Nice try, Mom, but my miniature Washington monument and Grand Canyon snow globe aren't going to change my mind about this place.

I toss my backpack in the corner; no need for that till Monday. After pulling on some athletic shorts I grab my phone and head downstairs.

Back in the kitchen, a plate of mouth-watering cookies and a glass of milk await me. Just like when I was five. No complaints from me, I'm starved after my questionable lunch.

"Thanks, Mom." I sit at the table to devour the still-warm chocolate chip cookies.

"Do you like your room?" she asks.

"Sure," I mumble with my mouth full.

"I thought I'd help you settle in, make it feel like home. Oh, I almost forgot, Rachael called. Did you remember tomorrow is the Special Olympics fundraiser?"

"Oh." I had hoped to somehow get out of it. Sure, helping kids who face different challenges is worthwhile, but I don't know if it's how I want to spend my Saturday.

"Rachael is counting on you," she adds, apparently sensing my hesitation. "And those kids will be thrilled to see you."

"Chill. I told her I'd go." At least I'll get to hang out with Rachael for the day. Besides, it'll get me out of this place.

Right then my dad walks into the kitchen to join us. I'm tired of them both working from home—never any alone time.

"Jake, I just got off the phone with your principal," Dad says, disapproval in his eyes.

Great.

"How can you possibly be failing after only one week?"

"What?!" Mom stares at me in disbelief.

"You haven't turned in one assignment," Dad continues.

"You've always been a straight-A student. What's the problem?" Mom asks as she sits down across from me, concern crinkling her forehead.

"Nothing. It's just stupid."

"Stupid is not having an education. You can't be a snowboarder forever," Dad lectures.

"There are other ways to get an education besides going to some worthless, small town high school."

"We talked about this. You're not getting a tutor," says Mom.

"No, you talked about this. You never listen to what I want," I snap.

"Hey, it's easy," Dad's voice strains with anger. "You either pull up your grades or you don't compete this season."

"What?"

"It's your decision," he states.

"I'm outta here." I shove my chair back, begin searching my phone for my playlist, and storm out—the door slamming behind me.

Needing to move, I start to run on a trail behind our house that leads into the woods, not caring where the path takes me.

Arrgh! My parents are obsessed with school. They're so sure they know what's best for me, they won't even listen. It's my life. I'm almost seventeen. I am totally capable of knowing what I need.

But, until I'm eighteen and old enough to move out, I'm stuck. Everything I've earned through endorsements and races is off-limits till I'm older. My parents' and lawyers' brilliant idea. Why do adults think they know everything? I'm the one who worked for that money.

Cranking up my music, I increase the pace. I can't believe they threatened to take away the one thing I care about. Total bull. Of course it wouldn't be hard to pull up my grades. School has always been easy for me. But I don't want to. I used to like school, but it seems pointless now. I've had a taste of a whole different life, and I don't want to be like everyone else.

Contemplating my problems, I charge through the forest of evergreens and aspens, not paying attention to my surroundings. Suddenly the thick bushes and tall trees disappear as I come to a clearing. Large mossy boulders and small green plants surround a small, crystal-clear lake. A rustic, hand-painted brown sign identifies it as Claim Jumper Creek.

I stop and pull my earbuds out; the extreme quiet is a shock to my system. The sound of the aspen leaves rustling in the wind, the creek gently cascading over rocks into the still water, and the quiet chirping of crickets replace the heavy bass of my music.

I wander around the picturesque pond shimmering in the afternoon sunlight, while a frog on his lily pad stares at me. Some kind of wildflowers line the water's edge, and tall pines frame the rugged mountain peaks in the distance.

This place reminds me of why I've always loved Colorado. The scenery is awesome. My parents enjoyed skiing and really wanted me to learn, so we drove out here a lot when I was a kid. I quickly became obsessed with the massive mountains. Kansas is ridiculously flat with its endless fields of corn, but this place is like another world with its rocky peaks soaring into the sky. All I wanted was to be outside, part of this wonderland, and snowboarding was one way to do that.

I sit down on a flat rock near the water and pull my shirt off to wipe the sweat from my forehead. The frog croaks at me like I'm disturbing him.

"Hey, buddy, I've got my own problems."

What am I going to do? I can't survive without snowboarding, but I don't want my parents to have the satisfaction of winning. There's got to be a way I can get my grades up without lifting a finger.

Suddenly my amphibious friend leaps in the pond. An eerie silence descends on the place as the critters all seemingly disappear. Do they know something I don't? I get a whiff of a weird decaying smell and can't shake the feeling that I'm no longer alone. A deranged ax murderer? Rabid bear? The ghost from the mine? As my imagination wanders, the disturbing silence is shattered by the snap of a branch.

Chapter 4

Sophie

What a mind-numbingly long week this has been. At least things did improve slightly from that first irritating day of school. A few of the kids have come up and admired my car. Chad even said it fit my personality perfectly. I'm taking it as a compliment even though I'm not quite sure it was. He either thinks I'm cute and spunky like my little bug or I remind him of a green insect.

But the best thing that happened is I figured out when to stop at my locker to avoid Mallory and the clones. And since they are always following Jake, when I avoid Mallory I also avoid Jake. Bonus.

At least the week will end with something fun: Kate and I are heading to Denver tonight to see a movie. We thought about going to the away football game, but we didn't feel like riding in a smelly school bus all the way to Idaho Springs. And our parents don't want us driving over Guanella Pass at night. Besides, our football team isn't exactly good, and it's completely embarrassing to always lose.

With time to waste until Kate picks me up, and because I'm tired of Everest following me around the kitchen with those sad puppy dog eyes of hers, I reach for the leash. She goes ballistic, whining and jumping around the back door. Everest can be very persistent or a real pain, depending on my mood. She's kinda like my brother that way . . . only cuter.

Once outside, Everest leads the way. With her nose to the ground she pulls me along. It's hard to tell who's walking whom. After a few blocks she veers into the woods, her favorite place. The animal scents make her crazy. What is it about eau du squirrel that dogs find irresistible?

Eventually we end up at Claim Jumpers Creek, one of our favorite spots. It sparkles like diamonds and is hidden in a dense forest surrounded by trees and mossy rocks. My own little oasis. Some of the best photos I've taken have been of the stream cascading down from Mount Thompson and emptying into the pond. One of my pictures even earned first place in a contest last year and now hangs outside the school library.

Tired of my arm being pulled out of its socket, I unhook Everest. With a low growl, she charges through the trees into the clearing, in hot pursuit of a grasshopper. I follow along, then climb on a boulder at the edge of the pond and watch her try to pounce on her prey. The gurgling mountain stream and quaking aspen are the only other sounds besides her splashes in the water. The peaceful setting makes this the perfect place to come when I have serious troubles and need to pray. No big dilemmas to solve today. This afternoon I can just enjoy the peace and quiet.

I close my eyes and take a deep breath, but the antici-
pated fresh mountain air is permeated with a putrid fishy
smell.

Ugh. What is that?

I glance over at Everest to see what she got into. But she's
innocently wading into the pond amid floating sticks and
leaves. The stream gently tumbles over the rocks behind her.
Slowly I focus on the debris in the pond which is shiny—with
scales and bulging eyes. My stomach turns as I watch dozens
of dead rainbow trout bob around her. Gross.

"Everest!"

She looks up, then splashes toward me bringing a whole
new disgusting scent with her. There's nothing like wet dog
with complimentary decomposing fish stench. Eww.

As I debate how to con Sam into giving her a much
needed bath when I get home, this weird prickly feeling
comes over me. You know, like I'm not alone. Before I freak, I
glance around hoping it's my overactive imagination. But my
eyes fall on a guy sitting on the other side of the pond watching me. My body goes cold; my heart leaps to my throat.

I stifle a scream. Come on, Sophie. Don't be afraid—the
Lord is always with you. Think. Panicking won't help. I reach
for my cell phone, thinking I'll pretend to call someone, then
I won't seem as vulnerable. But my pockets are empty. Of
course I left it at home charging. Brilliant. On to Plan B. I
start to climb down off the rock to grab my rancid-smelling
dog and prepare to hightail it out of there when the recogni-
tion part of my brain finally catches up. I know that guy. A
quick double-take confirms it. . . . Great. Jake.

What is he doing here? Just then Everest notices him too, and with her tail wagging furiously, she bounds around the pond. What a traitor.

Jake leans over to pet her. I try to get my heartbeat back under control from my near panic attack, but suddenly realize he's not wearing a shirt. Now my cheeks start to burn. As hard as I try to avert them, my eyes won't move. *Please, God, don't let my mouth be hanging open.*

The longer I stare at him, the more awkward the moment becomes. I try scanning my brain to remember the advice from any of the many online articles I've read, but I'm pretty sure "How to Talk to Arrogant Celebrity with Gleaming Six-pack" was never covered.

I come to the quick conclusion I'm going to have to go over and retrieve Everest because it's obvious from the way she's laying on her back getting her tummy scratched, she has no intention of leaving his side. He does have a way with females.

As I approach Jake pulls on his T-shirt. Not sure if I'm relieved or disappointed. Hey, annoyed or not, a girl can't help but be impressed by all those muscles.

"Hi," I mumble, noticing that the decaying fish smell isn't so bad on this side of the pond.

"Hi, I'm Jake," he smiles.

Gee, Captain Obvious, I had no idea.

"You're Sadie?"

"Sophie." And we've already met twice, you jerk.

"Oh. Sophie. And who's this?" He asks, indicating the extremely happy canine at his side.

"Everest. She's a Labradoodle, at the moment a very smelly one."

"She's cute," he says as Everest blissfully squirms around on her back basking in his attention.

"Do you come here often?" he asks with a grin that makes him look like he's up to something.

I control the temptation to roll my eyes at such a lame line. "Actually, yes. This is one of my favorite spots to come and think. I usually never see anyone here though." Especially creeps.

"I had to get out of my house," he confides, looking right at me with his piercing blue eyes.

I can't take the intensity of his gaze and glance away, trying to think of something to say. My eyes fall on the brown sign at the edge of the pond. "Do you know how this place got its name?"

He shakes his head, still watching me.

"Well, Claim Jumpers are people who would take over other people's property. There were a bunch of them around here when the town was first settled. They hung out, waited for the landowners to leave town, then took over the land. Supposedly this spot was where they liked to camp while they waited."

I glance over to see he hasn't taken his eyes off me. "There are lots of unusually named spots around here. Most of them have some story behind the name." Why is random information spewing from my mouth?

"You sure know your history," he finally says.

Is that a slam?

"My dad's a bit of a history buff." Silence. I guess he's not into history; probably just another subject for him to avoid.

"How did you get so good at snowboarding in Kansas anyway?" I ask trying to fill the silence, even though I already know the answer.

I read all about it in some magazine. How when he was a kid he begged his parents to let him snowboard. How that rush of adrenaline kept him pushing to the next level. He was such a natural his parents agreed to sign him up with a coach. Which meant for years each winter he and his parents, who were teachers, would leave their little Kansas town Friday after school and make the seven-hour drive to the mountains. Jake would do his homework in the car, then train all day Saturday and half of Sunday before they made the long journey back home just to make his dream a possibility. Actually, I read that article five times, at least.

He grins and, surprisingly for such a narcissist, says, "Lots of ski trips out here. And I'm pretty good with a skateboard too."

"Oh, skateboarding. I tried that once, and have the scars to prove it." I grimace as I remember my disastrous attempt. "I once begged my cousin to teach me some tricks. He made it look so easy. A chipped tooth and ten stitches on my knee later, I discovered how un-easy it really is. Not one of my finer moments." I shut my mouth, realizing I am talking too much . . . again.

He laughs, slightly tossing his head back. The afternoon sunlight filtering through the trees catches his mesmerizing eyes, with those ridiculously long dark eyelashes, making them sparkle.

"If skateboarding isn't your thing, what is? Everyone has something they're good at," he says.

"I'm the exception to the rule."

"I heard you're an excellent student."

"Yeah, I guess," I answer, surprised and—I'm embarrassed to admit—a little flattered he actually knows something about me.

"Hey, I was thinking maybe you could help me with my homework," he adds.

Ahh. It makes sense now; of course the only reason he knows anything about me is because it could benefit him.

"You want me to tutor you?" I can't help but feel smug. I knew this guy shouldn't be in my honors class.

"Not exactly tutoring. Maybe do my math homework *for* me once in awhile." He flashes his famous smile. This time it's not so alluring.

I stare at him unsure how to respond. Just 'cause he's gazing at me with the most stunning blue eyes I've ever seen doesn't mean I'm going to compromise my principles. Eventually I manage, "You want me to *cheat* for you?"

"My training schedule is extreme and I hardly have time to breathe. I'd be eternally grateful." He doesn't even acknowledge that what he's asking me to do is wrong!

"Why don't you ask Mallory?" I snap.

"I don't think she'd really improve my grade, do you?"

True. Maybe he's brighter than I thought.

"Well, will you help?" he asks.

I'm about to say, *"Listen, Casanova, I don't know why everyone thinks you're so great, but I don't. There's no way I'll cheat for you."* But then another thought crosses my mind. This is my golden opportunity to expose him for the liar and cheat that he is. I know it might be a bit deceptive, but isn't showing everyone this guy's true colors the more important thing? I push it out of my mind before my conscience gets the better of me.

"Maybe we could work something out," I answer instead.

He grins conspiratorially, not even caring that cheating is wrong and could ruin my reputation, not to mention any chance of getting into an Ivy League college.

Infuriated that there was never any doubt in his mind that I would agree, I reach over and attach the leash to Everest's collar.

"What are you up to this weekend?" he asks like nothing unusual just happened.

"Kate and I are going to a movie."

He laughs, "I suppose you're going to some chick flick."

"No," I answer emphatically, although that's exactly what we were going to see. "What's wrong with a romantic comedy anyway?"

"Nothing, they're just all predictable and totally unrealistic. Why do girls love to have guys do stupid romantic things? Wouldn't you rather have a strong, tough guy?"

"Oh, like some action hero? Yeah, that's really realistic. Most guys I know would never go out of their way to save a girl; they'd rather just save their own hides."

He smiles at me again, amusement twinkling in his eyes. This guy is exasperating. How does he keep his giant ego inside his pretty little head?

"Well, see ya," I say, making my exit before he can ask me anything else. It would have been a much more graceful exit if Everest hadn't dug her heels in the dirt trying to stay near Jake. Watch it, dog, or your days as my after-school companion are numbered.

An hour later I jump into Kate's car, hoping to get my encounter with Jake out of my head.

"Are we still going to see *Love, Forever and Always*?" Kate asks.

"No!" I say a bit too quickly. "I mean, I'm actually in the mood for an action movie."

Kate gives me a strange look. "Okay. Well, that will be fun too."

As we head out of town and approach the highway we see the tell-tale flashing lights of a police car.

"That deputy is at it again. Seems like every time I drive through here he's got some truck pulled over," says Kate.

"I know, he loves to sit in his speed trap. Don't mess with a man and his radar gun," I say, cringing at the memory of him pulling me over this summer, which of course reminds me of Jake.

"Hey, guess what Mr. Ego did."

"You mean Jake?"

"Whatever. I ran into him while walking Everest. He asked me to do his homework for him."

"You're kidding. What did you say? You weren't rude, were you?"

"No." Although I did ramble on like an idiot.

She studies my face. "You're going to do his homework?"

"No. I don't cheat." I don't tell her my plan. She'll only try to talk me out of it.

"It's a perfect excuse to hang out with him."

"Give me a break. I don't want to spend time with him! He's obviously not very bright."

"Geez, Soph, you act like you're sixty, not sixteen. Who cares if he's not smart? He's gorgeous."

"Looks aren't everything. What good is it to have a good-looking guy if he's a jerk? Jake Taylor just uses people," I say, then turn the radio on and crank up the volume.

Chapter 5

Jake

Although this Special Olympics thing wouldn't be my first choice on how to spend a perfect day like today, at least I have something to do. With the music blaring and the fresh air blowing around me, I drive up Hoosier Pass, through Pike National Forest, and over to one of the ski resorts in Summit County. I had to get away today. Couldn't take one more minute of being stuck at home with my parents. All this family togetherness is driving me crazy.

Rachael is emceeing the event and got my teammates and me to donate stuff for the auction. I gave her one of my practice boards. Only Rachael could talk me into these things. I'm fine with going, but I've never been to a Special Olympics event before. What do I say to them? Do they talk like regular kids? How do I act?

I'd pretty much do anything for Rachael though, and she knows it. She kept an eye on me at the Olympics. The guys all thought it was hilarious when I kept making rookie mistakes, like when I tried to check in at the women's site; luckily Rachael pointed me in the right direction. She always had my back.

I don't know what I'd do without my teammates. They're really the only ones who understand my insane life. They've all been through some of this before. Although unlike them, who had tons of attention before the games, all my craziness has come afterward. They're my only real friends, unlike those traitors Rick and Jon.

As I pull into the parking lot at the resort I'm amazed at how different the mountain looks without snow. The ski runs are now trails of green. At the base of the lift a giant tent is set up for the event. The place swarms with families and their special needs kids—everyone's happy. I smile, not sure how I'm supposed to act around them. Rachael said the Special Olympics is an organization for kids with intellectual disabilities, to help them grow in confidence. Sounds great but I'm not sure I'm the guy to help her. I don't want to screw up.

I make my way over to the check-in area, successfully avoiding talking to anyone. Thankfully the volunteer at the table points me toward Rachael, alone in a corner studying her notes.

"Jake! I'm glad you made it. Thanks for coming. I've never had to give a speech at one of these before. I could use the support," she says while nervously playing with her blonde curls.

"You'll be great. Why wouldn't I be here? You said there'd be free food," I say, trying to act cool and not like I'm totally out of my element.

"Man, they let anyone crash these things," says a voice behind me that I'd recognize anywhere.

I turn to see my teammate and the current Halfpipe Gold Medalist, Tommy Henderson, ultra cool as always with his spiky dark hair, goatee, and shades.

"Hey, bro. Didn't know you'd be here." Seeing another familiar face makes me relax. I turn to Rachael, "Did you bribe him to be here?"

"Are you kidding? I love these things. These kids rock," answers Tommy, high-fiving a little boy who walks by.

Just then a guy around fourteen or fifteen years old with Down syndrome comes up to us.

"Hi, Jake," says the boy.

"Hey, how are you?" I answer.

"I'm Mitchell," he says as he pushes his glasses up the bridge of his nose.

"Nice to meet ya, Mitchell," I say, shaking his hand. "Are you ready for a fun day?"

"Yep."

"Awesome. Well, good luck," I say and expect he'll wander off, but he keeps standing there. Tommy and Rachael really could jump in at any time now to help me out.

"We go to school together," Mitchell finally says.

"Really? You live in Silver Springs?" I don't think I've seen him around school.

"Yep."

"What grade are you in?"

"I'm a sophomore."

"Cool. Do you live in town?"

"No. We have horses."

"Sweet."

"Can I ask you something?" Mitchell asks.

"Sure."

Tommy and Rachael lean in close to eavesdrop. Don't they have somewhere to go?

"The girls at school like you." Out of the corner of my eye I see Tommy nudge Rachael. "I like this one girl. I don't know what to say to her."

Tommy jumps in, putting his arm around Mitchell's shoulders. "Oh, you need help with the ladies. Don't ask this dweeb. I'm your guy. What you need is a smooth line to get her attention. Like, 'Hey baby, where've you been all my life?'"

Rachael interrupts, "Mitchell, don't listen to him. Just be yourself. Walk up to her and be nice. Give her a compliment. Girls like guys who are sincere."

"Okay, thanks. I'll try. See you later, Jake."

"See ya at school, Mitchell," I say, impressed with how natural Tommy and Rachael were with him.

"So, what are we supposed to do around here?" I ask Rachael.

"This morning is all about having fun and playing games with the kids. After lunch we'll have the live auction and hopefully raise a lot of money for programs for them. For now, go join in the races and mingle."

Tommy says to me, "Let's go try the three-legged race, Young Gun."

The open space at the base of the ski runs near the ski village has been transformed. Various activities are set up amid bouncy houses and face-painting booths. We walk through the crowd over to the roped off race course. Tommy immediately teams up with some ecstatic kid. I try to look inconspicuous, wondering how I'm going to make it through the day.

A tiny girl standing alone a few feet away catches my eye. The referee hands her a piece of ribbon but she has no partner, and her big brown eyes start brimming with tears. I keep expecting someone to come up to her but no one does. She glances around while her bottom lip starts to quiver. Oh, man, even I know what the right thing to do here is. I take a deep breath, then walk over to her.

"Hey, I'm Jake. Would you be my partner?" I ask her.

She looks up at me with a shy smile and nods.

She takes my hand and we make our way to the bright balloons at the starting line. After tying our legs together we line up with the other twosomes. The whistle blows and we stumble forward. Her small legs and my long ones are totally uncoordinated and she keeps tripping. She looks at me, tears on the brink of spilling down her freckled cheeks. Oh geez, not the tears again.

"No worries," I say as I put my arm around her waist and hoist her up. I awkwardly lope toward the finish line with her on my side. We break through the streamer, seconds before the other groups. We don't get the first place ribbon since we didn't follow the rules, but we do get the teamwork award. My young partner wraps her arms around my neck. Her grateful mother has to pry her loose.

Tommy and I both join the sack race, but he totally sabotages my victory by plowing right into me. The kids think we're hilarious. The rest of the morning flies by with other field-day-type games.

"See, I knew you'd have fun." Rachael walks up to me after a tough tug-of-war battle. "Aren't the kids great? They get so excited about their accomplishments."

"Yeah, their enthusiasm is contagious."

A clanging bell indicates lunch is about to be served.

"Enjoy lunch. I'll see you at the auction," Rachael says.

"Good luck."

At the food tent, I line up with everyone else. As I wait someone taps my arm. When I turn around a small redheaded boy and his parents smile at me.

"Hi. You guys having a good time?" I ask.

The boy nods, his huge eyes staring at me.

"This is Noah. He's one of your biggest fans, Jake," his mother says.

"Very cool." I squat down to be at his level. "Where are you from, Noah?"

"Montana," he whispers.

"A friend of ours told us you'd be at this event and we drove all the way hoping to meet you," Noah's dad explains.

"Wow. I'm honored." They drove that far to meet me? I hope I don't disappoint. "Maybe we can sit together at lunch," I say to Noah.

He beams.

We pile our plates with burgers, potato salad, and watermelon, then sit together at the end of a long table covered with a checkered table cloth. Noah doesn't say much but he never stops smiling.

"You were incredible to watch at the Olympics," Noah's mom says after they tell me what else they've done on their trip to Colorado.

"Thanks. It was awesome to be there," I answer.

"I still remember how shocked everyone was when you qualified for the finals," Noah's dad says.

"You must have been so nervous," Noah's mom adds.

"Yeah, but since no one thought I'd be a serious contender, I didn't have much pressure on me. I think that's why I did well. I just went out and had fun."

"That last run you took," continues Noah's dad, shaking his head. "I've never seen anything like it."

I grin remembering the final round. I threw down my best run ever, hitting the Blindside 1260 perfectly and nailing the double cork. My mom thinks God was guiding me. My coach says I peaked at the right moment. Who knows? But I do remember the crowd going totally ballistic. I was sure the scoreboard was jacked up when it showed I had earned the highest score yet of the competition. Un-freakin'-believable.

"Well, it certainly was exciting. You deserved it."

"Thanks, but I was lucky. Hey, Noah, what do you like to do back at home?"

"Fish."

"No way. I love to fish. You and I have a lot in common. Do you also like ice cream?"

He nods.

"How 'bout we go check out the sundae bar?"

He nods excitedly and scurries to the dessert table. I have to hurry to keep up with him.

Following lunch, the crowd moves to the auction area. Rachael gives her speech and thanks everyone for coming. Don't know why she was nervous. She's a natural. After huge applause she hands the mic to the auctioneer.

I stand in the back and watch the bidding. When my board goes up on the auction block, Rachael pulls me on stage. I hold the board, doing my best game show model imitation. My Montana friends start to bid on it but eventually stop as the price rises. Noah's smile disappears.

After a photo op with the highest bidder, I jog to one of the nearby shops and buy one of the resort's baseball hats. With a permanent marker I find on the nametag table, I write a note on the brim then sign my name. As the bidding starts on an autographed hockey stick, I make my way back through the crowd to find Noah and his family.

"Hey, buddy," I say kneeling down next to him. "I had such a fantastic time with you today. I wanted to give you something." I hand him the hat, and his smile returns.

"God bless you, Jake," his mom says. When I stand up she hugs me almost as tight as her son did. "He'll always treasure this."

"My pleasure."

Hours later Rachael, Tommy, and I crash on some sofas in the lodge, surrounded by huge pine beams and a massive stone fireplace. A day of games, autograph signings, photo ops, and demonstrating items for the auction has taken its toll. Who knew schmoozing could be this exhausting?

"Thanks, guys, for helping out," Rachael says without opening her eyes.

"It was fun. You were right, the kids are awesome. I can't explain it. They were all so. . . nice," I answer.

"It's called being genuine. Hard to come by sometimes."

"Glad you raised so much money. No need to thank me," Tommy jokes.

"Of course, it wouldn't have been possible without you," Rachael says, then turns to me. "His ego needs stroking at least once a day."

"How's the new town and school treating you, School Boy?" Tommy asks me.

"It's lame. But there are some cute girls to help pass the time."

"Good boy, you learned from the master."

"There's also an abandoned mine that's just waiting to be explored."

"Nice! All right, my work here is done. Excuse me, I need to go check on that pretty ginger over there." Tommy makes his way over to the grand staircase and a beautiful redhead.

"Somewhere under that playboy façade is a good guy. On days like this he proves there's hope yet," Rachael says as she shakes her head. "Tell me, what do you have against your new high school?"

"Who cares about football games and pep rallies? It's stupid," I answer.

"One day you may wish you had experienced all that stuff. I missed my senior prom and still regret it."

"Really?" I find it hard to believe. She has such an amazing life.

"Jake, you can't snowboard forever; be careful not to throw your life away. Lots of child stars and athletes lose their way. They get caught up in the fame and the party scene and ruin their lives. That's why I choose to focus on how I can give back and help others."

"When did you become such a mother hen?" She's starting to sound like my parents.

"I was about your age when my snowboarding career started to take off. It was great because my friend Emma Jacobson started to rise in the field as well. We were thrust into the spotlight together. And our lives changed. We both began to party with some of the older athletes. For whatever reason, I didn't get as much into it as Emma did. She soon got really messed up with alcohol and drugs. One night after one of those parties, she and two other boarders, all completely stoned, were driving through the mountains and crashed. None of them survived."

I'd heard about that accident; the coaches love to scare us with that story. I didn't know it was Rachael's friend though.

Rachael continues, "Afterward I realized that I can decide to enjoy this gift of being an Olympic athlete. Not many people are blessed with these incredible opportunities. That's why I volunteer with Special Olympics. I've been trying to use my fame, while it lasts, for good. And to save your pretty little face," she adds, grinning at me.

"Thanks for the warning, but it doesn't mean that what happened to your friend will happen to me," I finally say.

"No, but the path of fame is filled with people who only want to use you. It's easy to start believing in your own greatness, but don't let the fame change you. It's important to find people that are real and pull us back down to earth when we get too full of ourselves. We're lucky to have gotten where we are, but it can be gone in an instant. Then who's left? All those fame seekers or the ones who truly care for you?"

"All right, I'll think about what you said. If you promise to stop the lecture."

"Deal," she says as she throws one of the couch pillows at me.

"I better hit the road," I say as I gather my stuff.

"Thanks again for helping out today, Jake. You were great with the kids."

"It was awesome. Keep me posted on other events, I'd definitely help again. See you soon. Can't wait to get back to training."

"Don't remind me. I think I'm getting too old for this." She groans and leans back on the couch.

"Yeah, twenty-four's pretty ancient."

The rest of the weekend is spent under house arrest. Not only am I being punished for my less than stellar grades, but my parents weren't happy that I ended up getting home two hours later than they'd expected. So I spend most of my time alone in my room or lifting weights in the basement. Anything to keep the interaction with my parents to a minimum.

No matter how loud I crank the music I can't stop the continuous loop of thoughts running through my mind. Probably because of Rachael's sermon.

Numero Uno

—I keep thinking about Mitchell. He's obviously seen me and thinks I'm the go-to person for advice about girls. But I never even once noticed him around the school. . . . I'll have to look for him this week.

Dos

—Something one of Mallory's friends said at lunch the other day has been bugging me. It was a simple question but I can't get it out of my head. She asked what my hobbies are. Hobbies? Do I have any? What do I do in my free time? When was the last time I just hung out? Before the Olympics all my time was spent training. Afterward it was all travel, interviews, and endorsements. Summer was spent moving. Snowboarding used to be my pastime but now it's my life. What does that leave me with? Music and my jeep? Shouldn't life be about more than that?

Tres

—Even if I did have something to fill up my ridiculously boring days in this place, who would I do it with? My snowboarding buds are all in their twenties. And none of them live nearby. It's not like we can go chill. Maybe I need to rethink my not-getting-involved-with-the-community plan and get to know Chad or ask Mallory out.

Cuatro

—Is this what suddenly having too much time on my hands does? Makes me analyze everything? Thanks, Rachael.

So, as pathetic as it is, I find myself actually grateful to get to school on Monday morning. Unbelievable.

Between my first and second classes someone yells, "Hey, Jake!" in the middle of the crowded hallway. I turn to see Mitchell, frantically waving his arms above his head to get my attention.

"Hey, dude," I holler back, ignoring all the stares.

Wonder if I've walked by him every day and never noticed him before. Well, those days are over. That's not who I want to be . . . plus, I don't think he'll ever let me pass unnoticed again anyway.

In class, I pay a bit more attention. Just enough to make sure I don't fail. One thing's for sure, I've got to get my grades up. I can't lose my snowboarding privileges. But I refuse to try very hard. And hopefully the Ice Princess will make life easier when she does my math for me.

That's one girl I can't figure out. Everyone else around here falls all over themselves for me, but not her. Although she did stop scowling at me long enough during English to tell me she's usually at the town library in the late afternoons if I want her assistance. No idea why she agreed to meet me, but hey, I'll take what I can get.

On the way to the lunchroom a framed photograph on the wall causes me to stop. It's a picture of the pond I found on Friday. Next to it is a photo of an old wooden structure set in a rocky hill.

"They're good, aren't they? One of our students took them." I turn to see Mrs. Alvarez, my English teacher.

"I was there the other day," I say, nodding to Claim Jumpers Creek.

"You haven't made it up to the mine yet?" She gestures to the other photo.

"That's the Silver Springs mine?"

"Yes. The road up is a rough 4-wheeling one. My son used to love taking his truck up there. It would be perfect for you and your jeep."

Who knew she was cool? "Thanks, Mrs. Alvarez. I'll check it out."

Maybe it's time to actually explore the mine. Forget my mom's concerns; a little danger and adrenaline rush might be just what I need.

I enter the nearly empty lunch room; somehow I always seem to be one of the first to arrive. I gather my tray of unrecognizable and horrible smelling items, then sit at my table. Chad strolls in and grabs his food. I wave him over.

"Hey, Chad, grab a seat."

"Cool."

Soon a few of his buddies join us.

"I was wonderin', was it like crazy when you got back home after winning the silver?" asks Chad.

"Insane. I had no clue that I had become an instant celebrity until I saw my face on all the magazines at the airport."

"Hey, I heard you started on a skateboard," says a guy named Dylan.

"Yeah, a couple of buddies and I used to spend all our time riding at a skate park."

"Sweet. You gotta join us, man."

"Sounds cool."

For once, lunchtime flies by as we share stories of epic wipeouts.

At the end of the day, not ready to head home, I climb in the jeep determined to find the 4-wheel drive trail to the mine. I was planning on inviting Mallory but she's busy with cheerleading practice. Seems everyone around here has a life but me. After twenty minutes of driving around the outskirts of town, I finally find one dirt road that looks promising. But part-way up the trail, a huge black pick-up truck with Texas plates and a large skull and crossbones sticker in the window blocks the path. I don't see the cowboy pirates around, and since there's no way to edge around the truck due to the thick trees on either side, I finally give up and turn back for home.

Chapter 6

Sophie

After visiting football practice with Kate to take pictures for the yearbook and learning our team's lofty goal this year is to win at least one game, I head to the library. I haven't told Kate the real reason I've been going to the library more often than usual is to implement phase one of my Bring-Jake-Taylor-Down plan. So far though, he's been a no-show. And since it's Friday afternoon, I'm sure he won't make it again.

The town library is located in one of the area's original buildings, down the street from the Cold Rush. Silver Springs looks like something from a Hollywood western, with a jailhouse, saloon, and a few other wooden structures. As you walk down Main Street, you kind of expect some gunslinger to start a shootout at any moment. The library building was the original mining company office. Of course its interior has been remodeled over the years, but the outside has been carefully preserved. This town loves its Old West history and has kept Main Street looking like it got lost in time.

The old wooden sidewalk that runs down Main Street was refurbished last year for fear of someone falling through the rotting planks. Any new business along this central thoroughfare has to be built with the same rustic look. I suppose Silver Springs is a lot like other touristy towns in Colorado that cling to their Old West heritage. The difference is we don't have many tourists crowding the streets.

Deputy Grady leans with his shoulder against one of the doors to the library, his back toward me, talking on his phone. Geez, could he be more in the way?

"Why are you worried? He's just some punk kid," he says.

My ears perk up. Someone's busted.

"No, it changes nothing. Don't worry. I'll keep an eye on him."

I wish I could stay and find out more, but I'm a little conspicuous standing here on the boardwalk eavesdropping. Bummer—it would be fun to uncover a good scandal.

I pull open the heavy doors and enter the large, book-filled room. The afternoon light streaming in the giant picture window creates long shadows that stretch across the room. Along the back wall is a big stone fireplace. Comfy couches sit invitingly in front of it. Dark paneling lines the rest of the space.

There are only a handful of people in the library when I enter. No sign of Jake again. This place can get pretty busy except on Fridays. Then the only kids here are some nerds who have nothing better to do. A few locals browse the shelves in search of a new book to read. I spot my mom by the periodicals.

"Sophie, I'm glad you're here," she says when she sees me. "I have some items I need to put in your car. I walked here this morning so I don't have mine. It's just a few boxes of books. Come on, grab a box. I'll help too. "

I'm about to groan at the thought of manual labor when Deputy Grady comes up beside us.

"I can put the boxes in her car," says the deputy. "Nice to see you again, Sophie."

"Really? Wow, that's great. Thanks, Deputy Grady," I say, surprised by his offer.

"Oh Lee, that would be wonderful. I have a couple of boxes of books to sort through," she says to the deputy.

"Isn't he the best?" she adds to me.

Yeah, as long as he's not giving innocent drivers speeding tickets, he's a gem.

I just nod.

"It's all part of my new Neighbors Helping Neighbors program. We should all be looking out for each other as much as we can in this town. I'm just making the rounds and seeing where I can help out," he explains.

"Well, I know the business owners around here appreciate your efforts," Mom says.

"My car's out front," I say, handing over my jingly keychain to him.

He turns and walks to her office.

"Can you do me another favor, Sophie? On your way home can you stop by Mrs. Meyers' and give her this?" Mom asks, holding up a book on veterinarian medicine.

"What's wrong with Duchess? I thought she made it home safe and sound after she went all rogue last week."

"She's been sick ever since she got back. Probably has something to do with the dead bird she dragged home with her. Anyway, the vet has run some tests but isn't sure what's wrong, so Mrs. Meyers wants to do some research on her own. She wants to learn more about avian diseases."

"She thinks Duchess has the bird flu?"

"Just be a neighbor helping a neighbor and take the book to her, please. I'll put it on your front seat."

I watch as she follows Deputy Grady into her office to get the boxes of books.

The peace and tranquility of the library is suddenly disrupted by loud shouts on Main Street. The front door flies open and Jake bursts in, causing heads to turn his way. I stand there and stare at him. Does he seriously have no library etiquette? He looks around, probably confused by all these books. Maybe I should explain these are what people who belong in my honors English class read. When his eyes fall on me his shoulders relax.

"Sophie," he pleads as he hurries over to me, "you gotta help me. I'm being followed."

Startled, I grab his arm and pull him with me through the rows of shelves. We hide behind the large reference section. I assume it's the paparazzi chasing him. Those stalker-ish reporters haven't descended on Silver Springs yet, but I've read how awful they are. Actually, I've been anticipating this sort of thing now that Jake lives here.

I try to figure out our next defensive move from these so-called journalists, when through the large front window I spot a herd of third grade boys stampeding down the board-walk. They are yelling to each other, obviously looking around for something . . . or someone.

I turn to look at Jake. "You're running from a bunch of eight-year-olds?"

The rambunctious group starts to point at the library and clamors toward the door, ready to enter.

Jake looks at me. "They scare me. Can you please help me out?"

I can't control my amusement and burst out laughing. Local stud, Jake Taylor, hiding from a bunch of kids. As ridiculous as it is, I really don't want the mini-cyclones charging through the library. I know how much of a mess little boys can make. And I do *not* want to have to spend my afternoon straightening up the library. So I grab Jake's arm again and pull him down an aisle as the boys burst through the library doors.

As we reach the side of the room I push on a corner of the chair rail; a section of the paneling moves inward, revealing a secret passageway. I yank Jake through with me and close the door behind us.

Total darkness engulfs us. I feel Jake tense up, obviously surprised by my choice of hiding spots. Belatedly I realize I'm in a pitch black room, inches away from this incredibly cute guy who smells unbelievably good. Wonder if he'd mind if I buried my face in his chest and inhaled.

"Great. I'm glad I followed you." Sarcasm drips from his voice.

"Fine," I say, snapping out of my momentary weakness. "You can go back out there with your little groupies." Some thanks I get for helping him.

"No, no, thanks for hiding me. I just wasn't expecting . . . this," he says.

I force myself to move away from him and shuffle toward the center of the space with my open hand searching the air. When I feel the dangling cord I pull and the small alcove is bathed in yellow light.

"Whoa, what is this place?" Jake asks as he looks around.

What was I thinking? I've never shown *anyone* my secret spot. And now I've ruined everything and shown Jake Taylor of all people. He stands there watching me as panic inches up my chest.

"Well," I quickly answer, my words stumbling out of my mouth way too fast, "Silver Springs was an old mining town. Of course you probably already know that. Anyway, the mine owner was this eccentric man who built tunnels that connected the town with the mining shafts. This building was originally his office, and he would take the tunnels into the mine to check on his workers."

"Sweet. I can't believe it hasn't all collapsed by now."

His blue eyes seem to bore right through me. What is it about this guy that makes me so nervous? Self-consciously I pull my arms closer to my body, hoping I don't start to sweat. Pit stains would be mortifying. Of course, standing in this enclosed space alone with him isn't helping the situation.

"Lots of mine shafts have collapsed," I explain as I break eye contact with him, "and most of this one probably has too, but parts of it have been kept up and even updated over the years. Rumor has it, back in the Prohibition years, the mayor used these tunnels to smuggle illegal items into town. When the sheriff would come searching, the mayor would also use it as an escape route."

Great, I'm talking too much again.

"Where does this one lead?" he asks, still intensely watching me.

"There are actually two paths. One leads through the base of the hill we are on and ends at a hidden exit down past the high school. The other leads up into the mine, although that one has been closed up for years for safety reasons."

"Can you show me the tunnels?" asks Jake.

I know I should say, *"No, tour's over. And if you mention this to anyone I'll hurt you."* But I find myself weaken again as I look into those hypnotic eyes, and instead I say, "Sure."

Carefully opening the secret panel, I peek to see if Jake's young fans are still in the library. The tranquil room is evidence enough that the gang of eight-year-old boys is no longer snooping around. Mom and her new bud Lee are out by my car, loading it with boxes. I hurry into the office, grab the key for the passageway, and jot a quick note to let my mom know I'll be back soon.

Suddenly it hits me. What the heck am I doing? Why am I showing him another one of my favorite places? He already knows about my pond, now this. But it's a little too late now for clear thinking. Where was my rational side ten minutes ago? Way to go, Sophie, letting pheromones cloud your judgment. I suppose the nice thing to do would be to show the new guy around, but this spot is mine and I don't want to share it. The problem is I've already said yes, so I brace myself for an afternoon of Mr. Perfect undoubtedly talking non-stop about himself.

With a glance around to see if anyone is watching, I push on the corner again for the panel to open. Jake leans against the wall, his dark hair framing his perfect face, grinning at me. Dang, this guy is hot—which really is part of the problem. Thanks to Jake Taylor I have a theory about cute guys. I don't trust them. Their good looks make it too easy for them to get everything they want in life. And because things have always been given to them, I believe they're never satisfied and therefore always looking for excitement.

"Okay," I say, and shake away my thoughts, "ready to see Silver Spring's big secret?"

He nods and I unlock a door at the end of the hallway. As I pull a string, one lone lightbulb illuminates the wooden staircase heading below the library. We carefully make our way down the narrow steps. The temperature drops as we head underground, causing me to shiver. A musty, earthy smell rises up to greet us. When we reach the bottom of the stairs the passageway forks and I lead us to the left. Lightbulbs dangle every few feet, giving enough light to reveal the chiseled stone walls and dirt floor.

Jake hasn't said anything yet as we make our way down the stairs and into the tunnel. I glance at him, curious what his reaction will be.

"Sweet," he says. "When was the electricity added?"

"Sometime in the '60s, the mayor at the time enjoyed giving tours of the mine and passages," I explain. "He wanted to leave everything in its original form as much as possible, but did add some modern touches."

Stop talking so much.

"Does everyone know about these tunnels?" he asks as he rubs his hand along the rugged walls.

"Yes and no. Everyone knows they exist. There are plenty of stories about their use. But most people think they were completely closed up years ago. It wasn't until my mom took over the library and had some remodeling done that the secret passageway was discovered. We showed the mayor and sheriff, but decided to keep it quiet so people wouldn't start using them." *Lord, I know you'll guide me always, but right now could you just guide my mouth to stay shut?*

As we walk, I sneak another glance at him. I can't believe I'm alone with him. *Again.* I mean, look at him—all tall, dark, and handsome. Definitely not my usual way to spend an afternoon. Determined to act natural, I decide to stop rambling and let him take the lead, but he seems perfectly content walking along in stony silence. Eventually the all-encompassing quiet gets to me.

"You grew up in Kansas?" I ask. Really? Who doesn't know that? He probably thinks I'm a complete idiot.

"Yep, in a tiny town. Sorta like this place but not as scenic, only corn fields on the horizon. And no awesome hidden tunnels."

"Do you miss Kansas?"

"Not really."

"Your whole town must have been excited when you went to the Olympics."

"Yeah, these two buddies of mine threw me an Olympic-size party when I made the team. . . ." He grins as he remembers, then his smile fades and he quickly adds, "But I don't have any friends there anymore."

"Oh." Strange. "What about relatives?"

"No. My parents are from Michigan. They moved to Kansas after college when they both got teaching jobs at a small high school. My dad taught accounting and my mom art. They liked it and decided it was the perfect place to raise kids, so they stayed. Now you know my life story."

I already knew it.

I rack my brain to think of something else to ask him to keep this conversation going, when surprisingly he shifts the subject from himself to me.

"Are you a Silver Springs native?" he asks.

"No, we moved here from Denver. Before I started kindergarten my dad finished his medical residency and we moved here. With the town nestled at the base of Mount Thompson, I liked to think the mine looked like a guardian angel perched high above."

Why do I continue rambling? Talking with a cute boy really shouldn't be this difficult. Maybe there are some online courses on how to converse with members of the opposite sex without totally embarrassing oneself.

"Do you know how Silver Springs got its name?" I blurt out. Here I go again.

"From the type of mine it is?"

"No, most people think it was a silver mine but it was actually a gold mine. You can spot gold mines by the yellowish streaks outside their entrances. Silver mines leave a grayish tint from their silt. Silver Springs actually refers to the way the fool's gold in the rocks shimmers in the nearby streams when the water flows over them in the sunlight. Personally, I think it looks more like diamonds. But Diamond Springs doesn't sound as good." I bite my lip and wonder if there is a medical term for diarrhea of the mouth.

He grins at me. "I like it. Diamond Springs adds a bit of intrigue to the town."

"Sorry to disappoint, nothing very intriguing around here."

"So who owned the mine?"

"Jeb McCarthy. He made his fortune when he discovered gold, but eventually the mine dried up and he moved on."

"Is Local Legends 101 a required course around here?" he asks.

He must think I'm a total loser, full of all this useless knowledge.

"No. My dad got really into the history of the area when we moved here and used to share the stories with me at bedtime." *Seriously, Jesus, help me shut my trap.*

"Is this where you bring all your guys?" he teases.

"No," I state emphatically. I can feel my face getting hotter. "In fact, I've never brought anyone here."

"Really? I feel honored."

"Don't. It was a momentary lapse in judgment."

He smirks, apparently finding my honest answer humorous. "Well, I can see why you spend so much time at the library."

"Actually, I don't come down here much anymore. When I was little and we first uncovered the tunnels I used to spend hours here. The reason I come to the library now is to volunteer. I tutor a few afternoons a week and run the story time once a month."

"Seriously, this place is cool. There's nothing this interesting back where I come from and no cool stories, only depressing dust bowl sagas."

"Hey, don't forget the greatest movie ever made featuring Kansas, *The Wizard of Oz*," I say in a sad attempt at witty banter.

"Yeah, the destructive tornados and green witch made Kansas look real appealing," he says sarcastically.

We reach the heavy bolted door marking the end of the tunnel.

"Well, Sophie, you're a fantastic tour guide," he says as we turn around. "Kind of like my own personal Colorado history app."

Super. What girl doesn't want to be compared to a cell phone program?

"I may need your expertise when I drive up to the mine," he adds.

I look at him as I try to figure out if he's being sarcastic or not. He's impossible to read though. "When are you going?"

"Don't know. I tried to drive up the other day but I'm not sure I found the right road. Mrs. Alvarez recommended the trail after I saw a photo of the place at school."

I stare at him. "I took that photo."

"Really? Impressive. I'm surprised."

"You're surprised I can take a good photo?"

"No. I just didn't know you were a photographer. You told me you didn't have any special talents, remember?"

"Oh." I forgot that snarky remark.

"Did you also take the photo of Claim Jumpers Creek?" he asks.

My cheeks start to burn as I remember our awkward encounter there. Not sure why *I'm* embarrassed when *he's* the one who asked me to cheat for him.

"Yeah, that's mine too."

"It's good."

Did he actually give me a compliment? Maybe he's human after all. That or he's just buttering me up so I'll do his homework.

"Thanks, I love it there. It's my favorite place when I need to be alone and sort through things."

"Is that what you were doing at the pond the other day? Contemplating the meaning of life?" he teases.

"No . . . just out for a walk. What about you? What were you doing there?"

"Actually, I was trying to figure some stuff out."

"Did you get the answers you were searching for?"

"Maybe, I'm not sure," he says, looking at me quizzically.

Uncomfortable with his gaze, I change the subject.

"Mrs. Alvarez is right. You'll like the mine. One of my favorite stories of Silver Springs is set up there. It's about Jeb McCarthy's daughter, Sally. She was what they called a 'Bloomer Girl.'"

"Bloomer Girl?"

"Yeah, some women ranchers and miners would wear men's trousers so they could ride horses like the men. Or sometimes they'd just take off their skirts and ride in their bloomers."

"Oh, tough chicks—like you."

"Gotta be. Someone had to save you from that wild pack of eight-year-olds. So why were you running from them?" I ask smirking.

He looks away. Finally he lets out a big sigh. "I guess I just wanted to be alone without anyone hounding me for something."

His seriousness stuns me. I thought Mr. Popular liked all the constant attention.

Soon we make it back to the stairs that lead up to the library. I stop, turn, and give him my best stern-teacher look.

"I seriously have never shown anyone these tunnels before. Not even Kate, and she's my best friend. If you blab, I'm going to have to hurt you."

"Scout's honor," he says and holds up the middle three fingers of his right hand.

I lock the door behind us. Then we sneak back through the hidden library panel.

"Are there any maps of the mine?" he asks.

"Yes, there's a copy here and one in the mayor's office. It shows the original plans of the mine, an entrance on the far side of the mountain by the mill, the tunnel into town, and the mine shafts. Do you want to see it?" I ask, again not sure why I'm going out of my way to help him. But I show him the maps anyway and even make a copy for him. All while ignoring my mother's curious glances.

"See, here's the tunnel behind the library," I say, pointing at the map. "We walked this way away from the mine. The other way leads you to a transport tunnel through the mountain and up to the main entrance."

"Sweet."

"It's totally boarded up now, so don't get any ideas."

"My dad read a story in the paper about some hikers claiming they were chased from the mine by a ghost. They were exploring the inside of the mine, weren't they?" he asks.

"I can't believe that story's still in the news, it's so ridiculous. All entrances to the mine have been sealed for decades. Those guys were camping outside the mine entrance. They drank way too much and scared themselves with ghost stories."

"Too bad. It would have been fun to explore. Well, thanks for the copy. I leave for L.A. tomorrow, so this will give me something to look at on the flight."

"Why are you going to California?" I ask.

"Oh, some sponsorship work and I have to attend the Kids' Favorites Awards."

"Tough life."

"Someone's gotta do it. Thanks for all the info. And for protecting me from the rug rats."

"You know where to find me the next time you need to be rescued."

"I'll keep that in mind." He grins and heads toward the door. He stops, turns around, and adds, "This was a really wicked afternoon, Sophie." With that he walks out of the library.

Oh wow, he said "wicked" . . . that means he *really* enjoyed himself. I hope Mom's not watching me, because I can feel myself blush.

Chapter 7

Jake

Saturday morning and Mom and I are sitting at Denver International Airport waiting for our plane. I hate to fly. Actually it isn't the flying part I despise but the hassle of parking, shuttle buses, and security lines. If I could access my money I'd charter a plane. Then I'd like traveling. Despite the headaches, I'm pumped about going to California. Can't wait to get out of Silver Springs, meet some girls, hang out at the beach. Just have fun.

Once we're at the gate, I lean back in my seat and listen to my music. A boy sitting across from us stares at me. I give him a half-smile and a nod. With his eyes glued on me, he carefully reaches into his backpack and pulls out a magazine. Uh oh, I've been spotted. I try to slump down and look inconspicuous but it doesn't help. He flips to a page, then looks back and forth between me and the photo spread. His eyes widen and he taps his dad on the arm, showing him the discovery. The girls sitting behind them must have overheard the conversation because they turn around to look and discuss as well, in turn causing others to whisper and point. I could walk away and come back later, but maybe Rachael's right. Maybe I should be using my popularity for good. The little boy who innocently began the whole spectacle approaches me with his magazine.

"Excuse me, sir. Are you Jake Taylor?" he asks.

"Yes, I am," I reply with a smile as I pull my ear buds out.

"Can I please have your autograph?" he says and hands me the magazine open to my photo.

"Sure, what's your name, buddy?"

"Charlie."

I'm not sure what to write. I used to always sign, *Stay cool,* but my conversation with Rachael bounces around in my head and suddenly that sounds too shallow. What would a good role model write? Eventually I come up with, *Follow your dreams.* Not sure that's any better.

Soon other passengers surround us and kids line up for autographs. My mom gives me an understanding smile as she gives up her seat for a young girl who wants her photo taken with me. Eventually we're saved by a flight attendant who leads us onto the plane and to our seats.

I settle into the window seat in hopes of avoiding any more attention. Closing my eyes, I try to take a nap, but all I can think about is yesterday's adventure with Sophie. For once I wasn't completely bored out of my mind in that town. Exploring those tunnels was awesome. Really, one of the coolest things I've ever seen. And hanging out with the Ice Princess wasn't so bad. She was even somewhat friendly—didn't glare at me once. In fact, she's pretty cute when she's not scowling. Though every time I looked at her she would jump into tour guide mode and tell me some story. Making her nervous really is too easy. I get a kick out of teasing her, and her local tales are actually kinda interesting. Maybe this town isn't completely lame after all.

✳

The restaurant at our hotel is very angular and modern. The maître d' leads us to our table, where my agent, Bill, sits with drink already in hand. When we approach he rises to greet us.

"Jake, Marcy, good to see you," he booms as he enthusiastically shakes my hand and kisses my mom's cheek. "How was your trip?" Bill's large personality makes him appear bigger than he really is.

"Everything was fine," Mom answers as we sit down.

"Are you ready for a busy week, Jake?" Bill asks.

"I'm ready."

"First of all, congratulations on being nominated for Favorite Athlete of the Year. The awards ceremony will be fun. I'm sending a limo to pick you up tomorrow evening to take you in style. The rest of the week is full; no time to play tourist. I've got interviews lined up, photo shoots, product endorsements. You'll be busy."

Not looking forward to the photo shoot. Trying to look cool is surprisingly difficult when people keep running up and placing you in awkward positions, fixing your hair, and don't even get me started on the absurdity of being forced to wear makeup.

"Oh, and I brought you a gift," he says as he pulls out a tiny digital camera. "I remember you said you like to take photos when you're on the mountain; this should fit in your pocket nicely."

"Thanks, Bill. It's perfect. I know I'll use it a lot."

"Jake, how are you liking the new school?" Bill asks after he places our order.

"It's school," I answer. Out of the corner of my eye I see my mom shoot me a look.

"As long as he doesn't fail, he'll be fine," she says.

"Jake, you've got to keep those grades up and stay out of trouble. The sponsors love your clean-cut image. You're a good role model for all the youngsters out there," Bill adds.

"No worries," I say, contemplating doing the stupid homework myself. I'm beginning to regret asking Sophie to do it for me after she was so cool yesterday and showed me that secret tunnel.

"Marcy, I want to give you a heads-up about the awards ceremony tomorrow. Family members are dropped off at a different entrance and have to sit toward the back of the auditorium. The night is all about the nominees. They get to make the grand entrance and are seated up front. When the camera shows the audience they only want to see celebrities."

"I certainly wouldn't want to ruin the shot," Mom answers sarcastically.

Works for me. Hard to meet chicks when your mom is sitting next to you.

I'm famished by the time the waiter places my dinner in front of me. Seriously? That's it? This has got to be the appetizer. But no, the miniscule serving is my dinner. I must hand it to Bill though, my petite steak is excellent. I could go for a couple more of them. When we finally get back to our room, I'm still hungry so we order room service.

*

My heart pounds as the chauffeur opens the door of the limo. When I step out of the car the crowd of tweens starts to scream. I really need to invest in some earplugs. While cameras flash around me, I wave to the fans. Blinded from all the flashes, I try to make my way down the red carpet without tripping.

"Jake, how does it feel to be up for Favorite Athlete?" asks a reporter as she shoves a microphone in my face.

"Awesome. I'm honored."

"Jake! Give us a pose," yells another one.

After a quick photo, I keep moving toward the door and away from the red-carpet insanity.

"Jake, no date tonight?"

"No, not tonight."

"Jake, who are you wearing this evening?"

I pretend not to hear that one, since "Whatever was in my closet" probably isn't the right answer.

Once safely inside the crowded lobby, I pass through security and am escorted to my seat, in the "celeb" area. As we enter the sprawling theater I recognize singers, actors, and fellow athletes. With this many gorgeous girls I should be able to find someone to hang out with this evening. The red velvet seats closest to the stage are labeled with the names of the nominees, indicating where we are to sit. My seat is on the aisle and, lucky me, I'll be sitting next to singing sensation Jasmine Humphrey. I'm about to sit when I notice her hourglass figure sashaying down the aisle. As she approaches I smile and try to act charming.

"Hi, I'm Jake."

"And?" she snaps, like she can't believe I would have the nerve to speak to her.

Not exactly the reaction I'm used to. Strike One.

She pushes past me and flounces into her seat.

The glimmering chandeliers dim, signaling the start of the show. Good, let's get on with this. The event is like every other awards show: emcees tell lame jokes, lip-synced musical acts perform, and lots of awards are handed out. Jasmine Humphrey wins for Favorite Song of the Year. As she makes her way to the aisle she practically skewers my foot with her stilettos. I manage a smile, not wanting the cameras to catch my grimace. Finally, my category is announced. I'm up against Spencer Ryan—a swimmer who competed in the Snowboard Cross and is now on some dancing reality show—and some motocross dude.

"And the winner is . . . Jake Taylor."

The audience cheers. I know it's just a dumb kids' awards show, but I'm stoked. It's always great to win. Somewhere cameras probably have a tight close-up of my face. Hopefully I don't look too dorky. Making my way up to the stage, I try not to trip over the cameraman awkwardly walking backward in front of me. Once on stage, I graciously accept the ice cream cone shaped award from the presenter then look out at the crowd. Whoa. This is one massive auditorium, full of people. All staring at me.

I try not to panic. Hey, Taylor, you won a silver medal, this should be no big deal.

"I want to thank all my awesome fans for voting for me. This has been quite a year. More twists than the double cork." Laughter. "Thanks for this award. You rock!" Then I lift the trophy thing in the air to loud cheers and applause.

The orchestra starts to play and I follow a pretty girl backstage to a backdrop where the winners are to pose for pictures. I wait as supermodel Aida Lewis, dressed in some feathery number, finishes her turn. She is obviously in her element as the cameras flash.

"Okay, Aida, how about a shot with you and Jake Taylor?" says one of the photographers.

Oh yeah.

"No." Her beautiful smile disappears. "My agent said I only had to pose four times." She spins on her four-inch heels and struts off in a cloud of feathers.

Strike Two. These California chicks are not easy to impress.

"I'll pose with Jake." I turn as teen superstar Celia Lawford swoops in and kisses me. The cameras flash. Whoa. Things are looking up.

After a few more pictures for the photographers where I try to look chill with the sultry blonde actress, we shuffle off as the newest winners come over for their photo op.

"By the way, I'm Celia," she says, leaning in close to me.

"I know. I loved your last movie," I say.

"And I loved watching you in the Olympics. You were incredible."

"Thanks. I'm definitely more comfortable on the half-pipe than at this awards ceremony, though. You're probably used to events like this."

"Usually they're a bore. But I think this one has potential," she says with a coy smile.

"I couldn't agree more."

"Well, what do we have here?" An older version of Celia in a clingy black dress with a plunging neckline walks over to us.

"Mom, this is Jake Taylor."

"Hi, nice to meet you," I say. Apparently she isn't stuck at the back of the theater with the other parents.

Mrs. Lawford smiles as she looks me up and down.

"Celia, you know the rule—save your flirting for those who can further your career. Teenage boys are off-limits."

Strike Three. I'm really on a roll.

"Of course, those rules don't apply to me," Mrs. Lawford says in a sticky-sweet voice as she sashays closer to me and runs her fingers through my hair. "You are even cuter in person, honey."

Oh boy. "Excuse me," I say and make a hasty exit from the crazy lady.

During a commercial break I'm escorted back to the auditorium. I'm thinking now that I won, Jasmine will be impressed with me, but the only time she smiles at me or leans in close is when the cameras are on us. Otherwise she turns away from me with her arms and legs crossed. Her music is good but her attitude stinks.

After a few more categories the show ends with a big musical number. Then the celebrities are escorted out of the theater and across the street to a hotel ballroom for the after-party. The planners must have raided a Christmas supply store from the looks of all the twinkling lights.

The deejay has the place rockin' with an innocuous mix of popular tunes. Waiters carry trays of mini foods and age-appropriate drinks. The cameras start flashing, taking "candid" photos that the photographers totally stage. "Lean closer." "Put your arm around her." "Come on. Act like you're having fun."

"Jake!" my mom finally finds me, rescuing me from the cameras. Good, now she can babysit my giant metal ice cream cone. "Congratulations! You looked so natural on stage."

"Thanks. I was really nervous. There were a ton of people in the audience."

"You handled it perfectly. Well, apparently I'm still not good enough to be seen in public. The chaperones are now banished—excuse me, encouraged—to stay in the back of the room. When you're ready to leave, you know where to find me."

"Okay, have fun."

"You, too."

As she leaves with my trophy in tow, a beautiful brunette in a skintight dress approaches me. She's about my age and looks familiar, but I can't quite place her. Some TV show? She's got a killer face but is so skinny I think she may blow away in the Santa Ana winds everyone keeps talking about. I have a strange urge to force-feed her.

"Jake Taylor. Yum," she says.

Did she just say "yum"?

"Having a good time?" I ask. What *is* her name?

"Not really; my friend and I are planning to ditch this G-rated shindig and go to a real party. Want to join us?"

"Maybe." Don't want to blow the first promising opportunity of the night. Just then her equally emaciated blonde friend joins us.

"Jake here might party with us."

"Ooo. Fresh blood." Her friend looks at me like she wants to devour me. "Can Courtney come?" she asks the brunette. "She always has the best stuff."

"Nah, she's back in rehab. Maybe next time."

"I think you're missing the point of rehab," I say.

They both stare at me.

"You know, no more partying?"

They burst out laughing.

"Gorgeous and funny too. Too delish."

"Seriously, stick with us. We'll take good care of you," says the blonde.

Chillin' with drug users is definitely not my scene. Besides, I hear Bill's voice in my head telling me being seen with these girls is not good for my image.

I leave the two of them so I can search for the buffet line. For some reason, talking with them made me hungry. After grabbing some hors d'oeuvres I look around, but don't see anyone I care to mingle with. This whole evening is not what I had expected. These people are complete phonies. I'm tempted to grab Mom and tell her I'm ready to go, but the thought of leaving a Hollywood party and heading back to a hotel with my mother is way too lame. So I wander around trying not to look like a total loner.

"Jake Taylor." My savior is none other than Dante Foxx, star of this year's hottest teen movie, "Alternate Dimension," and winner of tonight's "Favorite New Actor" award.

"Hey, Dante. Congratulations on your win tonight."

"You too. I'm sure tonight's trophy will look great next to your silver medal."

"It is quite the award."

"Could they come up with anything more ridiculous? You know, we have a mutual friend, Matt Brown."

"Oh wow, how's he doing?"

"Pretty good. He plans to be back competing this year. I think he'll be gunning for you."

Matt had actually placed ahead of me at the qualifying events last year and had earned the fourth spot on the Halfpipe Team. I was only there to "gain experience" but shocked everyone and placed fifth after the races, just missing the cut. But Matt took one more run to improve a move and crashed on the lip of the halfpipe, breaking his leg in two places. So I moved up to take his place on the Olympic Team. And the rest, as they say, is history.

"I bet he will. He's got a point to prove now. Man, I always felt bad that Matt's kamikaze run was my lucky break. No pun intended. How do you know Matt?"

"We grew up together in Salt Lake City. Hey," he says scanning the crowd, "want to get out of here?"

"Absolutely. You have no idea how much I would like that."

I follow Dante down a hallway and around a corner. The further we get from the party the less opulent the decor becomes. Finally we come to a service elevator. I glance around nervously waiting for someone to stop us, but the plain metal doors open and Dante pushes the button for floor 52, the top floor.

"A piece of advice: you need to stay far away from the Hollywood leeches," Dante says as we ride up the elevator.

"Are all the girls around here crazy?"

He laughs. "Not all of them, but I admit the cool ones are hard to find. Why do you think I still live in Utah when I'm not shooting?"

"Isn't that hard on the career?"

"It's a bit of a disadvantage to be away from the action of Hollywood, but I can't stand the phoniness. I like being near my family. They keep me grounded. Ya know, they're more than happy to tell me when I'm being stupid."

When the doors open, I follow Dante down another hall and up a flight of stairs, wondering where the heck we're going. Finally he stops in front of a metal door and punches in a code on the keypad. He pushes open the door and we step out onto the roof of the skyscraper. The shimmering lights of downtown L.A. surround us.

"Whoa."

"I know—rad, huh?"

"How do you know about this place?"

"I usually stay here when I'm in town and have made friends with the staff. This is where they come during their breaks."

Security gates keep us from exploring the rest of the roof but we can enter a basketball court, enclosed by clear walls. Dante picks up a basketball lying on the court and throws it to me. We play a little one-on-one, the unbelievable view of the city circling us. We shoot baskets until I try a three-pointer but totally overshoot and the ball soars over the clear wall, rolling across the roof until it bumps into the outer ledge of the building. I blame the dizzying height for my poor form.

Dante laughs, "Well, that's one way to ensure you don't lose."

"Didn't want to embarrass you."

"Hey, how's life in Colorado?" Dante asks as we sit on top of a picnic table at the side of the court and stare out at the sparkling city.

"It's okay. I wish I were in Vail or Aspen instead of some lame mining town, but it'll be nice to at least be closer to training."

"I think I'd choose the mining town over the ritzy resorts. As a matter of fact, I've been researching the Old West for a new movie I'm going to be in. This old guy told me about the '49ers code. Ever hear about it?"

"No."

"Well, during the Gold Rush when prospectors found gold, they sent messages back home to friends and relatives to have them come out and help them dig. Of course they didn't want just anyone to find out about their strike so they created a secret code. The problem was it took so long for the pony express to deliver the message and for it to be deciphered that by the time the family finally arrived, the site was often already taken over or proved to be a worthless claim."

"What was the code?"

"They'd send a map of the area but label it incorrectly. And the letter accompanying the map would be full of double meanings, providing clues to the exact location. For instance, the letter may say, 'You are right. We are all well.' That would mean turn right at the well. Or, 'Do not cave in to the pressure' would mean it's near the cave. I don't know how well it worked or even about the accuracy of the story, but I thought it was cool. The old guy I talked to swears his relatives were some of the lucky ones and made their fortune by using this code."

"I have a friend back home who would love this story. She's always telling me the local legends."

"Sounds like my kind of girl. Maybe I should be interviewing her for the movie."

"Yeah, she's pretty cool."

I can't believe I'm here at a Hollywood party, full of celebrities I thought I would have so much in common with, and I'm talking about Sophie Metcalf.

"Well, I think I've put in enough of an appearance," Dante says.

"Thanks for making tonight bearable. Tell Matt I'll be watching my back."

After exchanging phone numbers, we head back downstairs. Dante gets off at the floor he's staying on and I head back to the party. At least I met one cool person tonight.

Not wanting to deal with anymore of bizarro world, I search out my mom. Eventually I find her chatting with the bartenders.

"Jake, they were the only normal people in this place," she explains on our way toward the door. "I couldn't handle any more talk from the other parents about this audition, that acting coach, and who had what plastic surgery. Maybe next time you have one of these things I'll bring a book to read."

"Tell me about it. Maybe next time *I'll* bring a book to read."

"Jakey!" I turn to see the crazy duo I met when I first got here.

"Where are you going?" asks the brunette. "We've been searching everywhere for you."

"I left for awhile."

Mom shoots me a look.

"You promised you'd stay and party with us." The blonde pouts as she drapes herself on me. I can't help but notice the glassy look in her eyes.

"Sorry, girls, I'm outta here," I say trying to squirm away. Forget worrying about my image, these two are trouble.

The brunette shimmies up to me and sticks something in the front pocket of my jeans, then leans in, uncomfortably close.

"Give us a call while you're in town. We'll hook you up."

Embarrassed, I glance at my mom. She stares in disbelief at the whole spectacle.

"Come on, Jake. Time to go," she says and yanks me toward the exit. "What was that about?"

"Nothing." I look at the note they slipped me. Tiffani and Amber and a phone number. Now I know who they are—child actresses gone bad.

"They were on something."

"I know. Don't freak out. It's not like I'm going to do that."

"What did you mean when you said you left for awhile?"

"It's no big deal. I just hung out with a friend."

"I can't believe you snuck out of the party."

I can't believe she doesn't trust me.

She stares at me. "Jake, something's got to change. This new lifestyle you're exposed to isn't good."

"Mom, we've already moved to the most sheltered place in the universe. What more do you want?"

"I don't know. It's just . . . sometimes I miss our old life. No media, no agents, no unscrupulous Hollywood types, just the three of us having fun together. We had good people around us and a great church."

"Well, unless you can find a way to go back in time, this is our new reality."

"Don't get me wrong, I don't regret your success. You've been blessed with this phenomenal ability, but fame sure has an ugly side to it."

I hate to agree with her, but this really has not been the glamorous evening I had envisioned.

"Your dad texted during the party," she says, thankfully changing the subject. "He said the forecast calls for rain all week. They're expecting snow in the high country. Coach wants to take advantage and start training next week."

"Sweet."

"I know you won't feel like it, but that means you're going to have to go into school on Friday to turn in your homework and get some more for the following week."

Silver Springs High agreed to my modified schedule. When I'm away I work under my mom's supervision and turn in the assignments when I return.

"Fine," I answer.

Surprisingly, I'm not totally dreading going back to school. One thing I learned tonight is the Hollywood scene is not for me. Rachael and Dante are right—the glitz and glamour of being a celebrity is not all it's cracked up to be. This is not the life I want. I still don't know if I belong in Silver Springs either, but it feels a lot more like home than this place.

Chapter 8

Sophie

"Okay Sophie, hand over the remote," Dad says as he comes into the family room with his hand outstretched.

"No!" I stubbornly answer. "I'm watching the Kids' Favorites Awards tonight."

"Come on. It's Sunday night, time for football," he says as Mom and Sam enter the room.

Mom takes one look at my face then turns to my dad. "Dear, your team isn't even playing tonight. Can't you watch football downstairs? Sophie has been looking forward to this show."

"Fine," he grumbles and shuffles out of the room. Somewhere in the distance our phone rings. Sam starts to play in the corner with his action figures.

Maybe I should have gone downstairs where there was more privacy, but watching Jake on the big screen, hi-def set sounds way more appealing.

Mom walks into the room, extending her arm to hand me the phone. "It's Father Scott."

"Father Scott?"

"That's what I said," she answers, then returns to the kitchen.

What would a priest be calling about? This can't be good.

"Hi, Father Scott. Great homily tonight." I hope he doesn't ask which part I liked, cause honestly my mind kept wandering to the cute boy I hung out with in the tunnels on Friday.

"Thanks, Sophie. I was hoping to talk to you after Mass tonight but your family left right away."

"Yeah, we had a pressing engagement we needed to get home for." Which is about to start any moment. So hurry up, Father.

"Listen, I could use your help."

"Me? Help you?"

"Sure. I know you're in the same grade as Jake Taylor and I was hoping you'd show some leadership and invite him to join us one Sunday for the youth Mass."

My jaw drops. Hanging out with Jake one day was fine, but I'm not sure I want him coming to church and disrupting everything. Things don't stay the same when he's around and I like my parish just the way it is.

"Why me?"

"Mrs. Taylor came by the rectory and mentioned she'd like to get the family back to church but that Jake isn't all that enthusiastic. I thought an invitation from a classmate might do the trick."

"I suppose. But, do we really want all that extra attention? I mean, whenever Jake's around there seems to be a lot of unnecessary commotion."

"Sophie, I know you don't like change; I remember you weren't exactly thrilled when I first came to Holy Trinity last year either. But would God want us to close ourselves off or reach out to others?"

"Well, if you put it that way . . . "

"Try not to get too set in your ways or you may miss God's invitation to serve him."

"Fine, I'll invite him." How on earth am I ever going to find a way to bring that subject up?

"Great. Now I'll let you get back to your pressing engagement with the Kids' Favorites Awards," he says with a laugh.

Busted. "Oh. Um. Thanks, Father Scott."

I hang up just as the broadcast begins. One after the other, glamorous stars exit their limos and strut down the red carpet. The shot goes back to a limo being opened; my pulse quickens as Jake steps out. Oh.

He looks *amazing.* The crowd of girls screams as he waves to his fans. I close my eyes remembering how it felt to be inches away from Jake in the dark . . .

"Mom! I think Sophie's sick. Her face is all red!"

My eyes fly open to see Sam staring at me, and my mom hurries in from the kitchen. Her eyes go from my face to the TV and back.

"Sam, why don't you go watch football with Dad?"

"Okay. I don't want to catch what she's got." Sam loads up his arms with toys and heads out.

"Is Jake the reason you've been zoning out all weekend?"

"What? Hmm? Jake? I have no idea what you're talking about." I stare at the TV as Jasmine Humphrey makes her grand entrance.

"Well, I'm going to finish the dishes. Let me know if he wins."

She's right. I've been useless this weekend. It's been forty-eight hours since my big adventure with Jake in the tunnels, and I can't stop thinking about it. I keep replaying the whole encounter over and over. I mean, he was actually nice. He didn't talk about himself the whole time. He didn't ask me to break any more rules for him. In fact, we never even discussed his homework. And he even complimented me. Could I have misjudged him?

I was all set to write a scathing exposé, but now I'm wondering if maybe I was wrong about him. I don't know. There's no denying all those times I've seen him act like he thought he was better than everyone else. And he definitely asked me to cheat for him. But Friday in the tunnels, he was sweet and charming. He even said I should go with him up to the mine. Or something like that. I only wish I didn't get so nervous around him and babble incoherently. But even then, he didn't act like I was a complete moron; instead he asked more questions about the area. And now Father Scott wants me to invite him to church? I'm so confused.

Remember, Sophie, don't lean on your own understanding, but trust in God.

While the awards show continues I sink into the sofa and daydream about going to such an event with Jake, the two of us walking in together, arm in arm . . . cameramen snapping pictures of us . . . Finally, I'm jarred back to reality when *The Favorite Athlete* category is announced.

The screen divides into little boxes and each of the nominees is shown. Jake looks laid-back as usual, like he doesn't have a care in the world. How does he do that? I'd probably be puking in a bathroom somewhere.

"And the winner is . . . Jake Taylor!"

Of course he won. Big surprise there. I mean, seriously, who would beat him? Some motocross guy no one's ever heard of?

He smoothly makes his way on stage and says the perfect thing, being ultra cool and funny at the same time. Could someone like that actually like me?

❋

Monday the school buzzes for the entire day about Jake's appearance at the awards show. With everyone obsessing about it, I shouldn't have been surprised when an excited Kate calls after school.

"Soph, go check your email. I'm sending you a link to this awesome website. They posted all these amazing photos from the awards show last night. Jake looks unbelievably cute!"

"Maybe I'll look after I finish my homework," I answer. But the moment I hang up I bolt to the computer to see these "amazing" photos. I click on the link and, sure enough, Jake's handsome face pops up. The first photo is of him on the red carpet, his hair gleaming in the sunlight, a grin on his face. He has a hand in his pants pocket and looks completely relaxed. I quickly bypass the photos of other celebs. Another one of Jake comes up. He's holding his award up in the air after he had won.

As I continue to click through the pictures my happy mood starts to deteriorate. The next three shots are of Jake and Celia Lawford, practically on top of each other—of him with his arm around her, of her planting a big red kiss on his lips, and of the two of them looking longingly into each other's eyes.

The photos continue on at some party. I feel sick to my stomach as I come across several more shots of him. In each one, he is cozied up to some starlet, his arm around their tiny waists, them hanging all over him. I guess the airhead, fake-blonde, I-have-stuffed-animals-that-weigh-more-than-you look is his type.

What's the stupid saying my grandmother's always quoting? A picture's worth a thousand words? Well, these pictures tell it all, don't they? What a fool I am. How could I actually think he liked hanging out with plain old me? I can't believe I wasted a whole weekend daydreaming about him.

The weather during the next few days reflects my mood perfectly: gray, rainy, depressing. The thunderstorms continue most of the week. Not usual Colorado weather and completely disastrous for the hair. But spending so much time inside gives me a chance to reevaluate the Jake situation. I refuse to be like the other giggling girls in town. And there's no way I'm going to be used by some smooth talker trying to pass the time while here in Silver Springs. Back to my plan of showing Silver Springs the real Jake Taylor.

Finally, on Friday morning, I wake to sunshine. At my locker before class I overhear some passing sophomores mention that Jake's back. I see him briefly during English, but he stays after to conference with Mrs. Alvarez. She's probably showing him his failing grades. Good, shouldn't be long till he comes begging for my help again.

At lunch I grab my food and sit at a table to wait for Kate. Just as I stuff a fork full of pasta in my mouth I see someone, out of the corner of my eye, walk up to me.

"Hey, can I join you?"

It's Jake. Well, that didn't take long.

I try to quickly chew my mouthful of food without spitting it all over the table.

"Sure," I mumble, wishing I had the nerve to say, *"Why? Aren't there any dingbat blondes to keep you company?"*

He smiles as he sits down across from me. I expect him to hand over a stack of assignments or something, but he starts eating.

"So, you're back from sunny California?" Oh, brilliant deduction, Sophie.

"Did you miss me?" he grins.

"Nope. I enjoyed the peace and quiet," I snap, unable to control my mouth.

"It's good I moved to town then, to give your life some excitement."

"Yeah, I was lost without you."

"Exactly."

"Do you bug everyone like this, or am I the only lucky one?"

"You bring out the best in me," he adds.

"Fantastic. I see the trip wasn't all work. You managed to get quite a tan."

He answers with a grin, "Yeah, I spent some time at the pool; want to see?" He starts to pull his shirt up to show me those newly tanned, perfectly sculpted abs of his.

"No!" I quickly say, my cheeks burning. I hope no one saw that.

"Jake!" Mitchell Moore calls as he scurries over to us. For some reason he leans over and gives Jake this awkward hug.

Jake tenses up and looks around. Oh no, poor Mitchell. He's such a sweet, innocent kid and doesn't deserve Jake's jerky attitude. I'm prepared to tell Mr. Ego a thing or two on how to treat people when he shocks me.

"Hey, Mitchell. Have a seat. What's up, man?"

What?

"Hi, Sophie," Mitchell says as he sits next to me.

"Hi. How are your horses?"

"Good. Can you come and take their picture again?"

"Sure; next time you show them, let me know and I'll be there."

"You two know each other?" asks Jake.

"Of course we know each other. In case you haven't noticed, this town has like ten people in it." I roll my eyes at him.

"Sophie and I both helped at Vacation Bible School this summer," says Mitchell. "The kids all love Sophie."

"I bet they do," says Jake with a grin.

I scowl.

"I saw you on TV," Mitchell says to Jake.

"Yeah? Hey, did you ever get a chance to talk to that girl?"

"Jackie."

"Well, how'd it go with Jackie?"

"I got her phone number," Mitchell answers with a huge smile.

"Smooth, bro."

"We text now. Want to see a picture?" he asks as he pulls out his phone and shows us a photo of Jackie.

"She's cute, man."

"I gotta go. See you later, Jake. Bye, Sophie."

"Bye, Mitchell," I say, a bit bewildered by what I witnessed.

"Later," Jake says, then starts to eat again.

I stare at him.

"What?" His eyebrows furrow.

"I can't believe you actually talked to him."

Jake looks at me, confused.

"You think I'm that much of a jerk?" he asks, sounding genuinely surprised.

"You haven't shown that many redeeming qualities since you've been here," I answer.

Before he can respond we are joined by Chad, Kate, and Mallory—who plops herself next to Jake, totally invading his personal space.

"Tell us all about your Hollywood jaunt," says Kate as she settles in at the table.

"Well, we met some interesting people. Most seem to be waiting for their big break. One day we were in a cab on the way to one of the totally boring meetings we had in downtown L.A. The cabbie gets a call on his cell. As soon as he hangs up, he pulls over and tells us to get out because he's late for an audition. He drives off and leaves us standing there on the sidewalk, making us late for the commercial shoot."

"Dude, that's whack," contributes Chad.

"You shot a commercial?" asks Mallory.

"Yeah, for a jeep. Not sure why a snowboarder is driving on the beach, but whatever."

"That sounds so cool." Mallory's voice drips with envy.

"It was, for awhile. I was stoked about hanging out at the beach all day, but after about the twelfth take I was tempted to just go jump in the ocean."

"Did you go into Beverly Hills?" Mallory asks, tossing her long mane over her shoulder.

"No, but we did squeeze in a quick tour of Hollywood. Saw the Walk of Fame—where my mom took like a million pictures of Marilyn Monroe's star—and the La Brea Tar Pits."

"Oh, did you know over 200,000 fossils have been found in the tar pits?" I blurt out, remembering a report I did in sixth grade.

They all turn to look at me.

"Total buzz kill, Sophie," Mallory says.

"How do you know everything?" Jake asks.

I'm about to explain when Mallory changes the subject.

"What celebrities did you meet?"

Here we go. Now he can brag about all his starlets. But too bad for him, the bell rings. I take one last swig of my juice.

Jake stands up to leave, looks at me, and says, "See ya, Bloomers." Then he and Chad disappear.

Startled, I swallow wrong and start to choke. Oh no. He did not just call me that in front of everyone.

Mallory and Kate look at me strangely. Mallory storms off. Kate keeps staring.

"Did he call you 'Bloomers'?"

My coughing attack gives me a moment to gather my thoughts.

"Um, who knows?" I manage. Even if I wanted to explain the story of Sally McCarthy to her I couldn't, because I never told her about my excursion with Jake. Or about those darn tunnels.

"Is that some sort of nickname?"

"How do I know? He's weird." I grab my tray and hurry away, hoping she'll forget about it.

❄

"Sophie? Want to watch cartoons with me?"

"Sam, it's Saturday morning. I'm sleeping in," I mumble, my eyes still pasted shut.

"You already did. Now can you watch cartoons with me?" he sweetly asks.

"Fine. Give me a minute." After a night of watching our football team pull out a rare win and taking lots of awesome photos of the team and crowd celebrating, I had planned on taking it easy this morning. Still, I figure he won't stop pestering me till I give in, so I may as well get up.

I pull on some old baggy sweats, then head downstairs, plop on my favorite chair in the family room, and pick up my book. Sam sprawls out on the floor to watch his beloved cartoons. I can hear Mom in the kitchen doing whatever moms do. A perfect Saturday morning.

As I get to an exciting part of my book, the doorbell rings, interrupting the peace. Sam and I ignore it. Finally, Mom walks past us to answer it. I pretend not to notice the look she gives us. Engrossed in my book, I don't pay much attention but hear her chatting with someone. Sam on the other hand jumps up and runs across the room to the front window to check out our visitor. A glance at the TV reveals he left just as his favorite animated duo is about to solve their mystery. I can't help but be curious as to what could possibly be more interesting than unmasking a zombie. But before I have a chance to look out the window, Mom calls me to the door.

As I walk toward her, she gives me that questioning look of hers. What? I step out onto the front porch and come face-to-face with Jake. Stunned, I stand there staring at him. Here he is on my porch, leaning against the railing, wearing a

T-shirt, jeans, and expensive sunglasses. His baseball cap's on backward. Whiskers shadow his unshaven face.

Suddenly I'm aware of my incredibly frumpy appearance. This cannot be happening. Did I even brush my hair this morning? Thankfully I used mouthwash before coming downstairs. I stand there looking at him, trying to act like this is how I dress whenever I talk to boys on the porch.

"Hi, Sophie," he says.

"Oh, um, hi," I lamely mutter. "What are you doing here?"

Wow, Sophie, real smooth. Out of the corner of my eye I spy Sam staring at us.

"Well, I thought it would be the perfect day to go check out the mine," he answers with a grin.

"And you want *me* to go?" I ask, still not comprehending this situation.

"I was hoping you'd be my tour guide," he explains, glancing down at his shoes.

"A tour guide?" A tour guide *and* a "tutor." Here's the Jake I know and despise. It may sound like an innocent request, but I'm tired of feeling like I'm being used by this guy. The only time he comes around is when he wants something.

"Sure, let me change real quick," I say, not wanting to miss my golden opportunity to prove that I'm right about him. I turn back inside, forgetting my manners, and leave him standing on the porch.

Mom and Sam stand in the foyer watching me.

"What? The guy needs a tour guide," I say as I hurry upstairs to change.

❄

As we drive through town in his decked-out jeep, I feel a twinge of guilt.

I know I told Father Scott I'd invite Jake to church and I will, but showing people that Jake's a liar will actually help people. I mean, I won't totally ruin him, but I could save people a lot of heartache if they know the real Jake. All those starstruck kids would be spared the bitter disappointment of believing in an unworthy hero, and all the girls who dream of dating him would be able to guard their hearts. I could even help him realize the world revolves around the sun, not him. Yes, exposing him could actually be a service to both Jake and the community.

Zooming along in his jeep with the top off is awesome. I love the feel of the fresh air swirling around me. Good thing I put my hair up in a clip before we left. An old junky pickup pulls in front of us, forcing Jake to slow down. The whirling air sensation disappears. Bummer. No wonder he likes to drive fast.

I show Jake the turnoff for the 4-wheel road. As we head up the mountain, I play navigator and point out all the large boulders and deep gullies as well as the telltale mustard colored soil trailing down from the gold mine. He grins at me. Determined not to talk aimlessly today, I squeeze my lips shut. However, I can't help but sneak a peek at his biceps as he controls the steering wheel.

When we finally reach the top he parks near the entrance to the mine. Wobbly after the jerky ride, I exhibit my usual gracefulness and stumble as I climb out of the jeep. Jake grabs my arm to steady me and my breath catches. His warm hand gives me chills. Maybe this wasn't such a great idea after all.

"Hey, there," someone calls.

I jump. Deputy Grady walks toward us carrying a trash bag.

"Hi, I wasn't expecting anyone else to be here," I say, flustered.

"Just checking the mine, making sure it's secure. We sometimes have trouble with vandals and hikers. And today I guess I'm also Animal Control," he adds, holding up the trash bag.

"Why's that?" asks Jake.

"There were some dead squirrels lying around, but I think I got them all."

"Eww, that's weird," I say. "The other day we saw dozens of dead fish down at Claim Jumpers Creek as well."

"Maybe that ghost the hikers saw is killing them all," Jake jokingly adds.

"How does a ghost kill?" I ask.

"By scaring them to death."

I roll my eyes.

"You know, there could be something to that story," adds Deputy Grady.

"About ghosts? Don't encourage him," I plead.

"I'm just saying sometimes weird things happen. Maybe the spirits of the old miners don't like to be disturbed. It's probably best to stay away. Anyway, I'll check out the creek too. Jake, I didn't know you were back in town."

"I'm not here for long. Since there's good snow in the mountains we'll start training tomorrow, so I'll be away all week."

"What brings you kids up here?"

"I wanted to test out the 4-wheel trail with my jeep," Jake answers.

"Ah. There are lots of good trails around. You'll have to try out some of the other ones as well," Deputy Grady suggests.

"How did your squad car handle the hill?"

"The old logging road is easier on my chassis," he answers seriously, oblivious to Jake's joking tone. "I parked up top." He points out his car hidden behind some pines. "Well, I best be going. Stay out of trouble," he says as he walks up the hill.

I wave good-bye, keenly aware I'm now alone with Jake. My hands begin to sweat. I'm afraid any moment my mouth will start blabbing on its own.

"The view from here is amazing," Jake says, scanning the valley. "Wonder what the elevation is."

"It's 8,213 feet," I blurt out.

He looks at me with raised eyebrows.

"The only reason I know that is because my mom made it the alarm code at the library," I quickly explain. "Oops," I say, covering my mouth with my hand.

"Don't worry. I'm not planning on breaking in and stealing any books." He smirks, then heads toward the locked mine entrance, the only man-made structure left on the mountain.

Not knowing what else to do, I follow along. "I really wish I had my camera. I was hurrying so much I forgot to grab it."

"That's okay; I'll take enough photos for both of us," he says as he pulls out a tiny camera and snaps some photos of the Silver Creek Mine and, for some reason, me. Embarrassed, I turn away.

"You only like being on the other side of the camera?" he asks.

"Kinda." Something about him staring at me through the camera makes me uncomfortable, and my non-talking resolve is broken. "Why did you invite me up here?"

"I told you, I needed a tour guide."

"But anyone in town could have shown you the way. Why me?"

"Because you and your stories, Bloomers, make things interesting," he says as he rubs the back of his neck.

Is he making fun of me? I feel my face crinkle in confusion, which makes him laugh.

"Are you suspicious of everyone, or just me?" he asks.

"Pretty much just you."

"You know, I think I've figured out your problem."

"His name's Jake Taylor."

"I'm serious. You're kind of a control freak."

"I'm not a control freak." Am I?

"You like to have everything a certain way. You want your grades to be perfect. You don't like people disturbing your secret places, like the tunnel and the pond. You probably even have the next five years planned out."

"So? I'm driven and have goals I want to accomplish. You couldn't have gotten to the Olympics without being focused."

"True. I worked hard, but I also enjoyed the ride. Don't you ever want to stop planning for a moment and just see where the world takes you?" he asks.

"No, that sounds terrifying. I've realized I'm not a big fan of change."

"Like having me move here?" he asks with a grin.

"Precisely."

"My coach says sometimes you have to leap and try new things to reach your potential. I loved to snowboard, but if I never had the courage to try a trick on the halfpipe the first time, I would've been on the couch watching the Olympics instead of living them."

Seems like people keep telling me not to be afraid of change.

"I never did tell you about Sally and the mine, did I?" Eager to change the subject, I don't wait for him to answer before I plunge into the story.

"Well, one day her father, who owned the mine, had to leave town for several weeks. He left Sally, who was a teenager, and his foreman in charge of the operation. At first she stayed away from the mine. She didn't know much about mining so she left the details to the foreman. One day he came and told Sally the workers were slacking off in the absence of her father. They'd work in the morning then around lunchtime they'd meet here—at the top entrance—and spend the afternoon drinking. The next morning Sally grabbed her father's shotgun and rode her horse up here. Not sure if she wore her bloomers that day or not." I pause and Jake smiles.

"When she got up here she found all the whisky bottles lined up along this ridge waiting for the miners to take their afternoon break. Sally enjoyed some target practice and blasted the bottles away. The miners heard the gunshots and scurried out of the mine to see what was happening. She pointed the gun at them and told them if they continued to take advantage of the situation, she'd chase them out of town the same way she got rid of the whisky. She rode up every day to keep an eye on them, but they never gave her any more trouble."

"I could picture *you* doing something like that," Jake says.

"Yeah, right. Hey, speaking of Sally, she and her father were always worried that the mine would be attacked and chiseled some slits into the rock ledges up here. The small openings were just large enough to spy out of and to stick their rifle barrels through."

Jake searches along the mountainside near the mine entrance. "Have you ever found them?"

"No. I think the outside of the mine is too overgrown to see them, but you can find them on the blueprints I copied for you."

"See, that's why I invited you. No one else would've told me about that."

I can't help but smile. "Hey, that reminds me," he says. "I think I've found a piece of Wild West history that you may not know. Have you ever heard of the '49ers Code?" he asks.

"Um . . . no."

"It's something Dante Foxx told me about."

"Dante Foxx? You know Dante Foxx?" Wow.

"I ran into him at the awards thing the other night."

"That's right, he was there."

"You watched?" He asks with that mischievous smile of his.

"I mean, I heard that he had won something," I say non-chalantly, not wanting him to think I pay that much attention to his life. "What's this code thing?"

As we walk around the area, enjoying the view, Jake tells me about a secret code the miners used to tell their claim locations to trusted people.

"Wow, that's cool."

"I knew you'd find it interesting, Bloomers," he says with a grin.

My cheeks heat up.

"Why do you call me that?" I ask.

"I can picture you wanting to keep up with the guys and riding around in your bloomers."

"Oh. Do you have nicknames for all the girls?"

"What girls?" he asks. "Mallory?"

"Mallory, Jasmine Humphrey, Celia Lawford."

He chuckles and shakes his head.

Okay. That was totally stupid. Way to stroke his ego. Now he's going to think I'm jealous. But I'm not . . . right?

"Just you," he answers.

I blush and turn away.

❄

Sunday morning, Dad and I leave for the town of Breckenridge with a promise to Sam and Mom that we'll be back in plenty of time for evening Mass. Every winter, Dad spends several of his days off working as the ER doc at the ski resort. He doesn't need the extra work but enjoys the perks. Today he has a meeting with the other ER docs and the Ski Patrol. I always go along because his friend Big Jim, one of the managers at the resort, takes me around on his snowmobile.

As we cross the Continental Divide I'm surprised at how much snow the higher mountains have. No wonder Jake's coach wanted them to start training. Throughout the trip I try to sort through my feelings, but my thoughts just keep going in circles. I can't figure Jake out. Is he an arrogant jerk who uses people or is he a nice guy who, for some reason, wants to spend time with me?

All right, God, I know that inner voice that's telling me not to judge him is you. Help me listen. Maybe there's more to Jake than I thought.

We pull into the parking lot and park close to the front door. The resorts aren't open yet. There are only a few workers here, which makes the place unusually quiet. We climb the steps into the main lodge and Dad goes to his meeting.

Settling into a comfy chair in the lobby, I read while waiting for Big Jim. No sooner do I open my book than in he blows, his booming voice filling the room.

"Well, if it isn't the loveliest maiden of all." He picks me up and hugs me.

"Hi, Jim. I hoped I'd run into you today."

"Are you kidding? When I heard you were coming I put all my plans on hold." He sure knows how to make a girl feel special.

"I have a meeting later, but for now it's fun time," he continues. "Are you ready for our annual ride?"

"I even dressed for the occasion," I answer and twirl around, modeling my new white jacket with brown faux fur trim, matching boots, and white ear muffs.

He gives an approving whistle.

"Well then, let's go, little lady." He offers his huge arm to me and we head out of the lodge toward his snowmobile.

"Mr. Parker!" His assistant hurries after us. "The FBI called. The meeting has been moved up."

"Okay. Give me a call when they arrive."

"Did the FBI finally catch up with you?" I tease.

"If only it were that simple. Like the other resorts in the area, we've been having a drug problem the last few months. Our goal is to be a safe, family-friendly environment. This could be devastating for our business."

"Oh, that's serious."

"We're hoping to get a good lead on the situation before the season starts, but the FBI is having trouble tracking this ring down. But enough of my troubles, how have you been? You still planning to be a journalist and conquer the world?"

"Yup, I've been researching schools, and Columbia has one of the best programs. But it's super hard to get into and expensive, which means my grades have to be perfect."

"You know, I have a niece who's a reporter. She got a scholarship to college by uncovering some big scandal involving politicians. Maybe you could find an investigative report to work on."

"That's a great idea. I'll have to think of something. Thanks," I say, embarrassed about my juvenile image-destroying story on Jake that just yesterday sounded like such a good idea. Suddenly it's pretty obvious that using my gift to destroy someone would be wrong. But the thought of helping the community excites me.

We spend the next half hour flying up and down the ski runs on his snowmobile, the cold air whizzing past our faces. It's cool zooming along the hidden unmarked trails. In a few weeks all this will be filled with skiers. Big Jim shows me the new trails and snowmaking equipment. He tells me he's got a big surprise—the newest, most exciting addition to the resort. We cruise over a large ridge and come to an open bowl in the mountain. Big Jim stops the snowmobile at the crest of the hill.

"What's this?" I ask in amazement. There are rails and jumps, a halfpipe, and a few scattered snowboarders.

"We've redesigned our snowboarding park and invited the U.S. team to try it out today," he says, bursting with pride.

"The U.S. *snowboarding* team?" Nausea sweeps over me.

"No, the water polo team—of course the snowboarders. Aren't they incredible?"

Somehow he missed the dread in my voice. I'm not ready to see Jake again. I thought I had a whole week to figure out how I felt about him.

Panicking, I scan the area. Sure enough, there's Jake on the pipe; he's hard to miss with his signature bright green board. Flying up the side, he arches his back and grabs his board. He lands perfectly then flies up the other side, soaring ridiculously high above the edge of the halfpipe. I catch my breath as he rotates into a flip. I start breathing again when he lands safely and glides gracefully to the bottom.

"Come on, I'll introduce you," thunders Big Jim as he starts up the snowmobile again.

Chapter 9

Jake

Can't wait to chill with the team today. It's been way too long since we've all been together. Tommy, Max, Dan, and Rachael are standing around Tommy's truck when I enter the parking lot. I pull in on the far side of his red 4x4. The guys haven't seen my new wheels yet, and I enjoy the envious looks.

"Taylor," Tommy says, shaking his head as I climb out of the jeep. "You're the luckiest son-of-a—"

"Hey, watch your language in front of the kid," Max interrupts as he jokingly covers my ears. I elbow him in the ribs.

"Tommy, maybe if you cleaned up your image you'd score a jeep, too," Dan suggests.

"Nah, I'd make a perfect spokesman for a snowmobile," Tommy says.

"Hah! You'd be more appropriate for a speed dating service," counters Rachael.

"Hey! We can't all have a squeaky-clean image like Jake—that would be whack for the sport," Tommy says.

"You do have the whole rebel-without-a-clue thing down pat," adds Rachael.

"All right, you losers," Coach says, coming up behind us. "Let's get on the hill."

We carry our gear up to the main lodge while the General Manager of the resort comes out to greet us. "I'm glad you could come and check out our new and improved snowboarding park. Having the team test it is the perfect inaugural event."

These perks rock.

We jump on some snowmobiles and cruise up to the new area. It's sick. A slalom run, seven rails, four kickers, four jibs, and a halfpipe. This place is definitely not for the beginner. What a perfect warm-up to our training season. We take turns doing our favorite tricks and trying out all the different areas. The rails are a blast. It feels like forever since I've ridden, and I can't even remember the last time I rode just for fun. What an awesome day—perfect snow, deep blue sky, good friends. Life doesn't get much better. And like an idiot I left my new camera in the jeep.

After an easy sweep of the halfpipe to check out the snow, I decide to run it again, this time tricking it up a bit. Dang, I've missed this—the thrill of the speed, pushing the limits. I throw a giant backscratcher, nail the landing, pull an easy flip on the other side, then head down to the picnic tables with Max and Tommy for a break. I'm sitting on top of the table shooting the breeze with the guys when a snowmobile roars up behind us. Assuming it's one of the workers, I don't pay much attention.

"Wow, who's the Betty?" asks Tommy.

I turn to see Mr. Parker, one of the resort managers, with some chick. The snow bunny is decked out in a white jacket with fur trim, fur boots, and ear muffs. I do a double take because she looks a lot like Sophie. I know I can't get her out of my mind, but now every girl's going to remind me of her?

There's something about Sophie that intrigues me. She's an anomaly, not fitting into any of my Walker, Talker, Stalker categories. While I was in L.A. I kept thinking about that day she and I explored the tunnel. Then, on Friday at school, I walk into the lunchroom and as luck would have it, she's sitting all alone. Couldn't pass up such a perfect opportunity, but the conversation didn't go as expected. She seemed, well, kinda hostile. Then, unfortunately, the others joined us. Yesterday, I woke up and figured if I'm going to get to know her, I'd better do it. Being gone for weeks at a time puts me at a disadvantage, so I need to make the most of what time I've got. And it paid off. Yesterday at the mine was great.

I stare at Mr. Parker towering over his petite companion. Wait. That *is* Sophie. My pulse increases like when I make my first drop into the pipe.

"Sophie!" I call.

"Hey, Jake," she says quietly, glancing around at everyone.

The guys erupt in cat calls and howls.

"You two know each other?" asks Mr. Parker.

"We go to school together," she explains.

Mr. Parker's cell phone rings. As he answers it, I introduce Sophie to Coach and the team.

"Sorry to cut the tour short, Sophie, but I've got to head back for my meeting. Let's go," says Mr. Parker.

Sophie starts to climb back onto the snowmobile. My mouth starts running before my brain can filter my thoughts.

"Would it be alright if I take Sophie down later, Mr. Parker? I mean, she could stay with us awhile longer." Everyone just looks at me.

"I suppose that would be up to her," he answers. Now all eyes shift to Sophie.

I watch her look back and forth between me and Mr. Parker, probably weighing her options.

"I guess I have some time before I need to be back at the lodge," she answers.

I glance over at the guys. They shake their heads and smirk at each other. Great, I'm really gonna get smack now.

Mr. Parker gets on his snowmobile and with a wave pulls away. Coach and the others wander off, leaving Sophie and me standing there. What was I thinking?

"Are you stalking me, Bloomers?" I ask to break the ice.

"No." She looks offended, which cracks me up. She's way too easy to tease. "My dad had to come up here for a meeting, and I tagged along. I didn't know you'd be here. I thought you trained somewhere near Vail."

"Yeah, we do. But we couldn't turn down the invitation to check out this place."

"It is unbelievable," she answers, glancing around.

"Since you're here, you want to try it out?"

"The park? Oh . . . um . . . I don't snowboard."

"Have you ever tried?"

"Well no, but I think I'll stick to skiing. Remember my skateboarding trauma? I don't do boards."

"Come on, break out of that cautious shell and try something adventurous for once. Trust me. Rachael, do you have any extra gear Sophie could borrow?" I ignore the glare I receive from Sophie.

"Sure, she could use my old practice stuff. I brought extra equipment along in case the snow was bad," Rachael answers.

As she helps Sophie, she says, "Let me guess—Jake plays it super chill at school."

Sophie laughs. "Pretty much. I've only really seen him interact with the skateboarding crowd."

"And Mitchell," I add.

"Oh, is that the guy we met at the Special Olympics event?" Rachael asks. "He was awesome. That reminds me, Jake, the photographer sent me some photos I wanted to give you."

She digs through her bag and pulls out some pictures that she shows me. Sophie looks over my shoulder. There's one of me and my three-legged race partner bursting through the finish line, her face beaming; a few of Tommy and me during the sack race; and a great close-up of Noah and me.

"This one's great. Can I get a copy to send to Noah?"

"Sure."

"I didn't know you volunteered with kids," Sophie says, sounding shocked.

Rachael laughs. "Don't let his machismo fool you. He's really a good guy."

"Don't blow my cover," I answer. "Okay, ready to tackle the mountain?" I ask Sophie.

"I'm not sure this is a good idea."

We walk toward the magic carpet conveyor belt. "Hey, it's better than sitting in the lodge by yourself, isn't it?"

"I had a good book to read," she answers as we ride up the hill.

"Let me guess, a romance novel?"

"No. A mystery," she counters.

"With a romantic twist?"

Her frown tells me I'm right.

"Hey, no offense. I like mysteries too, but it seems most girls dig the romances."

Once we reach the top of the run she sits in the snow while I help her buckle into the board, then I get myself ready. I grab her hands and help her up. She wobbles, causing her to squeeze tighter. This was a good idea.

Slowly we move down the hill, me facing backward, gliding on my toeside edge, still holding her hands. I give her a few instructions and she slowly starts to get her balance. We spend about twenty minutes in our private lesson.

Finally, halfway down the run, she plops down in the soft fluffy snow, her dark wavy hair framing that beautiful face. She looks adorable.

"This is exhausting!"

"You're a natural." I pull out my phone and snap a picture of her.

"Hey!" She gathers some snow and throws a snowball at me. I catch it and toss it back at her.

To avoid being hit she leans sideways, which causes her to slip down the slope. I grab her arm to stop her but lose my balance and fall down too. We both start laughing, making the slide harder to stop. Finally, I manage to dig my board into the snow to stop us, but we end up tangled together—her partially under me, our faces inches apart, her beautiful green eyes looking up at me . . .

I quickly pull away and sit in the snow. "So, you come here often?" Real smooth, Taylor.

"Um, yeah." She giggles then readjusts herself. "We usually ski here. My dad works in the clinic sometimes and he's good friends with Jim Parker. Actually, this is where I learned to ski."

"I bet you were adorable with your little skis."

She blushes then changes the subject. "Do you know how this town got its name?"

"No." I lean back on my elbow, ready for another one of her history lessons.

"The man who developed this gold mining town decided to name it after then-Vice President John Breckinridge—with an 'i.' But when the Civil War broke out, the vice president joined the Confederate Army. The town was incredibly embarrassed and changed the spelling of the town to Breckenridge—with an 'e.'"

"What a scandal."

"I probably bore you with all these stories."

"Are you kidding? You and your stories fascinate me."

She blushes. "It's weird we ran into each other today."

"You can't mess with fate," I answer.

She smiles, then looks away.

"Hey, I'm impressed you gave snowboarding a shot. See, trying new things isn't so bad. "

"Yeah, it was fun, but I think I'll leave the boarding to you professionals," she responds, relaxing with a carefree laugh.

"I keep discovering your undisclosed talents: photography, skiing, tour guiding, dog walking. What other mad skills do you have?"

"I guess you'll have to wait and find out."

"Interesting proposition."

Her blush deepens.

"Well, I've already determined that you have the next five years of your life planned out. What does that entail?"

"I want to be a journalist," she says.

"I guess that fits with your control issues."

"What do control issues—which by the way I don't have—have to do with being a journalist?"

"In the past six months I've dealt with a lot of reporters and they all have an angle. They have papers to sell and viewers to grab, which makes them sensationalize every story instead of telling an unbiased truth."

"That seems a bit cynical."

"Have you read the stories about me?" I ask her. "No one can live up to all that hype. Why do you think I have to have such a squeaky-clean image?"

"To be a good role model?"

"Well, sure, there's that, but if I make one wrong move those same journalists that built me up will have no problem tearing me down."

"You go around worrying about that?" she asks.

"I don't worry. It's just the way it is. I'm not saying all reporters are bad. It's just there are two sides to every story, but usually they aren't both shown. So, when you become a famous journalist, remember not to control the story."

"I'll do my best," she says, looking at me oddly.

"Tell me, what did I miss at school last week?" I say, hoping I didn't just mess things up with her.

"Not much, except Mrs. Alvarez spilled coffee on her lesson plans one day so we had to watch an old movie version of *The Great Gatsby,* which isn't even on our reading list. I guess it was the only thing she could find in the AV room."

"That's exciting."

"Yeah, except just when I was really getting into the storyline, class ended and she didn't show us anymore of the movie. Now I'm curious as to what happens."

"What a shame. Will Gatsby win back the heart of the lovely Daisy or will she remain with her cheating husband, Tom Buchanan?" I ask in my most theatrical voice.

She stares at me. "You know *The Great Gatsby?*"

"Lots of audiobooks. Those long drives from Kansas to Colorado had to be filled up somehow. I would have preferred something from this century, but Mom always chose classics like *Gone with the Wind* and *Pride and Prejudice.*"

"If you've listened to them, then what do you have against romances? The strong tough guy can also be the romantic hero."

"They're not realistic. What regular guy acts like that?"

"When he wants to win the girl's heart he sometimes has to swallow his manly pride and show his sensitive side. Of course, I don't know any guy that would do that."

"Well, maybe if you added some food as an incentive you'd get better results," I joke.

"Oh, training guys is like training dogs?"

"How do you think I learned all those snowboarding tricks?"

She laughs.

"Ready to head down?" I say as I push myself up.

"No," she says, throwing her head back.

I reach down, pull her up, and then swoop her into my arms. I snowboard the rest of the way down the hill, carrying her. As I glide to the picnic table I glance down at her smiling face.

"I think I kinda like snowboarding after all," she says with a shy smile as I set her down.

"See, aren't you glad you stopped planning and just lived in the moment?"

"Yeah, I guess it was a good decision."

Then my testosterone must kick in because I head back up the hill to the halfpipe to show her what I do best.

With a wave to her, I push off, board down the hill then veer to the right side of the halfpipe to start the run. I turn and soar up the twenty-foot wall, flying another twenty feet above the lip. I start simple with a straight air grab. The air whips past my face as I fall back toward earth, making sure to hit my landing. Biffing it right now would be ultra humiliating. Landing smoothly, I fly up the other side, enjoying that familiar rush as I leave the wall and twist my body to rotate into the cork. The trees blur as I spin. My heart rises in my chest as I drop to the ground. I spot the landing then zoom across to the other side. Leaving the halfpipe lip, I grab the board and rotate so I have to make a blindside landing, my favorite. The risk of not being able to spot the landing is wicked. When I finish I ride up to her, spraying her with snow.

"Hey!"

The guys start to heckle me again for showing off. Who cares? I'll deal with them later. I take off my board, then reach out for her hand.

"Want to go for a walk?"

"Sure."

I take her mittened hand and we head toward a cluster of pines a few yards away. "You make it look easy. What was the last move you did?"

"It's called a blindside. The rotation of the trick makes it so you can't see the landing. You have to stretch and look over your shoulder to hit it correctly. I'm always trying to nail a perfect one. My mom calls it my signature move since it's one of my favorites. Although it makes her cringe."

"Looks terrifying."

"Just a little more practice and I'll teach you how to do it."

"First, I should probably learn to stand on the board by myself without resembling a bobblehead."

"I'll be happy to be your teacher if you want, Bloomers."

"We'll see. I liked meeting your friends. They seem really cool, especially Rachael."

"Yeah, she's like my big sister."

"I don't know how she deals with all you 'brothers.'"

I laugh. "I think she loves it. There are other coaches that work more with female athletes, but she seems to like training with the guys. Besides, someone's got to keep us in line."

"I can't believe I got to meet them all. I mean, I watched you guys on TV during the Olympics. It seems surreal to actually be hanging out with them."

"I know what you mean. I still remember the first time I met Tommy. I was stoked and completely in awe. Don't tell him, but I had his poster hanging in my room for inspiration. Now I know he's just a pain in the neck."

"Do you guys get to spend a lot of time together?"

"I wish. They're all a lot older. But it's cool to have friends who understand the craziness."

"My life has stayed pathetically boring this past year, while yours must have changed drastically," she says kind of surprised, like it just dawned on her that my life was completely turned upside down.

"Yeah, you could say that."

"That day in the tunnel, you mentioned you no longer have any friends in Kansas. What did you mean? You must have had a lot of friends."

"I guess I was referring to my two best friends, Rick and Jon. We used to do everything together. But after the Olympics they pulled a Jekyll and Hyde and blew me off. I think they were jealous."

"What happened?"

"When I first got back from the games things were cool. They helped organize this parade the town had for me. They even hosted a viewing party when I was on one of the late night shows. And of course they loved the perks, like when they got to sit in box seats for the opening day of baseball when I threw out the first pitch. But quickly they went from being stoked for me to being jealous. I remember this one night at the school basketball game. I was constantly surrounded by people asking for autographs, and those two ended up ditching me and leaving without saying a word. Another time, Jon was mad when I cancelled a fishing trip because of some interviews. But when I got back from the team's White House visit things really came to a head. I called them up to see if they wanted to do something. Rick said they were too busy. And that was it—they didn't talk to me anymore. I had all this attention around me but no one to hang with. I suddenly hated living there." I can't believe I shared all that with her. I've never talked about this with anyone.

"You know, you might have been acting like a know-it-all jerk," she tells me.

Whoa. "Is that what you think of me?" She said something similar at lunch on Friday.

"That's how you come across sometimes. Whippin' through town in your fancy jeep. Expecting people to want your autograph."

"But they do want my autograph."

"Yes, but don't assume they do. That's when you seem arrogant."

Wow. What do you say to that?

"Or, maybe you tailgated one of them and made them run a stop sign and get a ticket, thus getting grounded and having to pay the higher insurance rate out of her hard-earned savings."

Stunned, I stare at her.

"Personal experience?" I finally ask.

"Yeah." She shrugs.

"That's why you didn't like me?"

"One of the reasons."

"Sorry. I'm trying to work on controlling my speed."

"No, I'm sorry. I can't believe I said that. Here you open up and tell me about your old friends and I bring this up. That was completely rude of me," she says. "I have a terrible habit of judging people. I thought I had you all figured out . . . but I was wrong."

"Do you still think I'm an arrogant jerk?"

"Not any more. I guess I never thought about what you might have faced. I assumed your life was perfect. I'm sorry I misjudged you."

"You sure are different from anyone else I know, Sophie." She's always surprising me.

"Is that a bad thing?" she asks looking down.

"No. Actually, I like it," I answer with a grin while raising her chin, forcing her to look at me. "You keep me guessing."

She smiles. "Good. Someone's got to keep you on your toes. Can you send me the photo you took today?"

"Sure, I'll text it to you." We exchange numbers.

"I better head back down. My dad and I have to leave soon if we're going to make it back for Mass tonight," she says.

"Oh yeah, I almost forgot it's Sunday. You go to church in the evening?"

"It's the youth Mass. The praise music is fantastic and Father Scott is great." She closes her eyes like she's debating something, then adds, "You could come some time. Lots of kids from school go."

"Maybe, sometime when I'm in town."

"Not into God?"

"No, it's not that. We used to go to church all the time when I was younger. I was even an altar server. But once I began the snowboarding thing, we spent every weekend during the winter driving here. Then, when I went competitive, training picked up to pretty much year-round. It became harder to go, and soon we weren't making it very often."

"Ah, you're a CEO."

"CEO?"

"Christmas and Easter only."

"Pretty much," I grin.

"If you're ever around, come check out Holy Trinity. The youth group is great too."

"My mom would like that. She's been wanting us to go back to church."

"So, how do I get back to the lodge?"

"I'll drive you," I say and lead her to the snowmobiles.

I climb on one of the machines and she snuggles in behind me, arms wrapped around my waist. Halfway down the mountain, I realize her head's resting against my back. Too bad this ride can't last longer. As we pull up to the lodge, she straightens up.

"Jake, thanks for bringing me down. And of course the snowboarding lesson. It was really fun," she says as she climbs off.

She's right. It has been an awesome day. My confidence bolstered, I decide to make a move.

"Sure. Hey Sophie, I heard about this Snow Ball dance in town. If I'm not traveling when it happens would you go with me?"

Her huge green eyes and open mouth are priceless. She obviously has no idea how she makes me feel. Slowly she nods her head. "Sure."

"Great. And before you ask, no, I didn't ask anyone else. Just you, Bloomers."

She flashes her stunning smile as I pull away feeling invincible.

❄

Before heading toward Vail, where my mom is probably anxiously waiting for me at the condo we rent when we're in town, the team stops for dinner. The touristy section of Breckenridge has the same Old West feel as Silver Springs, just more happening. We burst into a local pizza joint like we own the place. One look at us and the hostess places us upstairs away from everyone else.

We spend the next hour reliving the highlights of the day. Max jumps on top of his chair to reenact Tommy's biff on his easy backside rodeo. In slow motion, Max contorts his face and body, mocking Tommy's dumb fall, eventually landing in a heap on the floor.

"Classic, Tommy," Rachael says. "What was with Coach? I thought we were there to have fun." She lowers her voice to a growl and gives a rockin' impression of the man. "That the best you got? What have you slackers been doin' all summer? Where'd you leave my all-stars? I'm going to be a laughing-stock! I give up. You guys can coach yourselves!"

"And what about Lover Boy here?" hollers Tommy as he slugs my arm.

He throws a napkin on his head, tucking the pretend locks behind his ears. Batting his eyelids, he leans toward Dan.

"Jakey," he says in a high-pitched girly voice, "you are such a stud."

"Why thank you, little lady," Dan answers, sounding more like John Wayne than me. He flexes his muscles. "Let me strap on my manly board and show you what I can really do."

"Oh, Jake."

"Oh, Sophie."

They embrace. The group roars. I throw a breadstick at them. Bring it on. Nothing they say can get to me. Today rocked. Spending time with Sophie was great. Of course she's cute, but there's more to her. She's interesting, smart, has strong beliefs, and is a little stubborn, but it all makes her intriguing. I wish I would've had the nerve to park the snowmobile, turn around, and kiss her right there on the mountain. But I probably would've scared her off.

After disturbing the peace long enough, we pay our bill and get ready to leave. As we thunder down the stairs, a guy at the bar catches my attention. Most people in the place are watching us—hard to ignore the commotion—but this guy is different. The skinny, greasy-haired dude is staring directly at me. More like, glaring at me. He's probably in his mid-thirties and looks kind of familiar, but I can't place him. Probably tailgated him, too. I really am trying to get better about that, but these people drive ridiculously slow. Whoever he is, he never takes his eyes off me until I'm out the door. Who cares? Nothing can ruin this day.

Chapter 10

Sophie

We make it back to Silver Springs in time for Mass, then head home for chili. Sam's freckled face lights up as he talks throughout the whole meal about his troop meeting. He shows us the emergency supply kit they made. It's full of bandages, a compass, a flashlight, flares, and everything else a good scout needs while camping.

Mom looks exhausted from her day with a group of rowdy boys. Normally I couldn't care less, but Sam's excitement keeps the conversation away from me and my day so I keep encouraging him with random questions, but don't pay any attention to the answers. Every time I close my eyes and remember how it felt when Jake carried me in his arms and snowboarded down the mountain, my heart does flips that rival what Jake does on his board.

I can't believe he asked me to go to the Snow Ball with him! And I just stood there with my mouth hanging open. He's used to being around super cool sports stars and Hollywood celebs. What does he see in me?

The other day he was so sweet to Mitchell. Today he was extremely patient with me during my snowboarding lesson. Around his teammates he was the one being teased. The cocky edge he usually carries around was gone. And seeing those photos of him with the little kids was touching. It was great seeing a more vulnerable side. He's totally different from what I thought he was.

I wish I wouldn't blurt things out without thinking, though. I couldn't believe he even opened up about his Kansas friends to me. And then I was completely rude. But Jake wasn't at all defensive like I would've been. He really is a good guy. And the strangest thing of all is—he apparently likes me.

And to think I almost jumped on that snowmobile and headed back down the mountain with Big Jim. I don't know what made me take the risk, but if I hadn't, I never would have seen this side of Jake. *Thanks, God, for opening my eyes. Please help me not to judge people anymore.*

"Okay," says Dad, jarring me back to reality. "My turn to choose the Family Night activity. Let's play Hearts."

I was hoping to go up to my room and daydream some more.

"Sophie, tell Mom about your day," Dad says as he deals the cards.

"It was good. Big Jim took me on our annual snowmobile ride."

The game gets going but all I can think about is how it felt to watch Jake on the halfpipe. Seeing him in person, effortlessly flying twenty feet in the air doing these insane tricks, I was mesmerized and terrified at the same moment.

"Sophie gets the queen! I won again! I'm really good at this." Sam can't control his excitement.

My head's totally not in the game.

"You seem distracted, Sophie," Mom says.

"I'm fine, just tired."

"I'm sure her first snowboarding lesson was very taxing," says Dad.

Real smooth, Dad.

"Snowboarding?" Mom asks.

"Cool!" hollers Sam.

"Jim took you snowboarding?"

"Not Jim," Dad adds.

I shoot him a look but he acts all innocent, shuffling the cards.

"Who?" asks Mom as she watches me.

I close my eyes and take a deep breath. "Jake was there with the team."

"No way!"

Why do little brothers have to yell everything?

"Oh, fun," Mom says cautiously.

I try a few more hands, but after my sixth straight loss I decide I've had enough.

"I'm exhausted. I'm going to go up and read."

"Okay, good night, dear," Mom says.

"Thanks for letting me tag along, Dad. Good night."

"Good night."

As I walk up the stairs, I hear the unmistakable sound of circus music. It gets increasingly louder as I approach my room.

"SAM!" I yell.

As I grab my phone, my annoyance vanishes when I see it's a text from Jake. I quickly pull up the text and a picture of me in my fur ensemble lying in the snow. I may not have been able to snowboard very well, but at least I looked cute trying it. Jake has written—

Here u go Bloomers. –J

J? Even his messages are cute. I make this photo the wallpaper on my cell phone. Just then my mom knocks on my door as she opens it.

"Hey, I didn't get to hear all the details of your day." So much for subtlety.

"It was fun." She's gonna have to work for this.

"That must have been a surprise to run into Jake." Here we go.

"Yeah. I met some of his teammates. Rachael Edwards lent me her gear so I could try snowboarding. I was terrible." Maybe I can change the subject.

"Wow. You've been spending a lot of time with Jake the last few days. Is he a nice guy?" Nope, right to the point.

"I think so. He's hard to figure out."

She laughs. "Welcome to the world of guys. They're always hard to understand . . . even after you've married one of them." Oh gee, that's helpful.

"Take things slow and be careful," she continues. Okay, here comes the lecture.

"I know, Mom." I can feel my eyes rolling.

"If you ever want to ask me something, I'm always here." I wonder how many times she's practiced this speech.

"Mom, I'm not even sure how I feel about him. You have nothing to worry about."

She thinks for a moment. I'm expecting some more nuggets of wisdom, but instead she says, "You know, Sophie, it's probably hard on him as well."

"Yeah, it's really tough to be famous, rich, and totally good-looking."

She smiles. "I'm just saying it's probably hard for him to figure out who likes him for who he is and who likes him only because he's all those things."

"I suppose, but how do I know if he's genuinely interested in me?"

"That's why I said to take it slow and be careful." Ugh. Fine, I get it. She leans over, gives me a hug, and kisses my forehead. "Good night, Sophie."

"Thanks, Mom. Good night."

The problem with parental advice is their experiences were so long ago they're totally irrelevant. I mean, my parents met in college, during biology class. They fell in love while dissecting a fetal pig or in some such equally repulsive, unromantic setting. What does that have to do with my situation?

With one last look at the photo Jake sent, I get ready for bed.

❋

A totally obnoxious sound jars me awake way before my alarm is ready to go off. I'm about to yell at Sam when I realize the crazy loud fog horn belongs to those dumb elk. Every fall their annoying mating calls draw visitors to the area. Realizing I won't be getting back to sleep, I go ahead and get up.

All day I catch myself zoning out in class. It could be because the bugling elk woke me at the crack of dawn. Most likely it's because I can't stop thinking about Jake. I just keep remembering how I felt when our faces were like an inch away from each other after my humiliating, uncoordinated slip down the mountain.

After school, Kate convinces me to photograph the cross-country team for the yearbook. Knowing that if I go home I'll only drive myself crazy, I agree.

The coach told Kate we should meet him at the corner of Long and Short at four o'clock. He'll be able to chat with us and I can take some photos as the team runs by. The intersection is not far from my house so I decide to drive home, change, and then walk Everest to the meeting spot.

As Everest and I are exiting our front door, Kate pulls up.

"I thought the plan was to meet there," I say as she climbs out of her car.

"I thought we could walk over together."

"Cool."

As soon as we start to walk, she pounces.

"What's going on with you and Jake?"

"What? What are you talking about?"

"My sister's hairdresser ran into her daughter's piano teacher who is married to the mailman who saw you and Jake together on your front porch Saturday morning."

Wow. I should've known this was coming. Secrets are impossible to keep in small towns.

"Um, who?"

"It doesn't matter. Is it true? Did Jake come to your house on Saturday?"

"Um, yeah. He wanted me to show him the gold mine."

"You went up to the mine with him?"

"He needed a tour guide."

"I thought you hated the guy. Now he's got a nickname for you and is showing up at your house. Is there something going on between you two?"

"I don't know. We keep running into each other and I keep babbling on about stupid history stuff."

We continue walking in silence. I feel her eyes bore into my head. Then she asks, "Anything else?"

"Well, I ran into him yesterday and he taught me to snowboard."

She keeps staring. "Very funny."

"No, really."

"You're serious?"

"Yeah."

She stops, grabs my shoulders, turns me toward her, and shakes me. "Why didn't you tell me?!"

"I don't know. I'm trying to sort out my feelings. He's totally different from what I thought he was. He has this sweet side I hadn't seen before. He's really a nice guy."

"So, you like him?"

"Yeah."

"Wow."

For some reason I can't quite bring myself to tell her he asked me to the Snow Ball. Why can't I share that with my best friend?

By the time we reach our destination, the cross-country coach is waiting along the side of the road. Kate walks up to him and starts jotting down notes as they talk. I take Everest and my camera across the street. While I wait for the runners I find a good spot to capture the action as they pass by.

"Sophie."

I turn to see Deputy Grady walk toward me. Everest lunges at him, barking ferociously.

"Everest!" I call, pulling her back.

She continues snarling and yanking on her leash.

"Sorry about that," I say to him. "I don't know what her problem is. She usually loves everyone." Stupid dog. How am I ever going to get on this guy's good side so he stops giving me tickets with her going all rabid-dog on me?

"I had to trap some raccoons earlier. They were getting into people's garbage. Maybe she smells them."

"Are they getting into Mrs. Meyer's trash again?"

"Yep."

Duchess can't even scare coons off. What good is that dog?

"What are you doing here?" I ask him, trying to keep my yapping canine at bay.

"Just helping Coach. I shut down the roads to make sure the team is safe."

"Oh, that's nice."

"Some days there's not a lot to keep me busy. I like to help out where I can. But when I saw you I wanted to give you this." He hands me some folded up papers.

"What's this?" It better not be a ticket.

"It's a printout of some other 4-wheel drive trails around the area for you and Jake to try. Since he's out of town, I'll leave them with you."

"Oh, thanks."

"Alright, I'll see you later."

Everest continues to growl until he climbs in his car and pulls away.

How embarrassing. Now Kate *and* Deputy Grady know about Jake and me. Not that there's much to know, but the way this town talks it's going to be hard to keep things a secret. I'm not sure I'm ready for everyone to know about us. Us? What "us"? I'm kind of getting ahead of myself here. It's not like we're a couple. But he did ask me out . . . .

"Sophie! You're missing the runners!" yells Kate from across the road.

"Oh, got it!" I say and begin to snap photos of the passing cross-country team.

❄

When I finally get home, I run up to my room and plop on my bed. I've been thinking about it all day, and have decided to make a bold move. I'm not going to wait for Jake to contact me. I'm going to text him back. After about forty-five minutes of debating what to say, I finally decide on the brilliant, *Thnx for the pic.*

An hour later while I'm doing my homework, my phone buzzes. It's Jake's reply.

Sure. What did u do today?

Okay, now what? Another lame answer would not be cool. Come on Sophie, think. Something witty. My mind flashes to the '49ers' messages Jake told me about. With a brainstorm, I type back.

Went to the old one-room.

A few minutes pass and I start to doubt my reply. He doesn't know I'm playing this game. He's totally going to think I'm an idiot. I'm about to text again and explain when the phone buzzes.

School. Good one, Bloomers.

Glad he got it. I quickly send another message.

How was your day?

The butterflies in my stomach go crazy as I wait for his response. I can't believe I'm doing this. It feels completely out of character. The phone buzzes. I grab it, then stare at his message.

Like this mountain range.

What does that mean? Oh. The Rocky Mountains? Finally, I type. *Rocky?*

Impressive, he responds.

You're just an old nail, I reply.

Yeah, a bit rusty.

Better get back 2 my hmwk.

I hate to let him go but don't know what else to say.

Me 2. syl.

I can't help myself and keep rereading our little texting dialogue the rest of the evening.

❄

Tuesday after school Kate insists we go check out a garage band. I don't understand why we're covering this because it's not a school-sanctioned activity. But as we walk into Dylan Robert's garage, all becomes clear. Chad is the guitarist. His smile to Kate gives it all away. I grin and raise my eyebrows at Kate.

"Hey, Kate, you made it," Chad says, flipping his hair out of his eyes.

"I wouldn't miss it," Kate says with a coy smile.

Apparently I'm not the only one with some secrets.

The guys play a set and their slightly alternative rock sound is actually good. Not sure if it's an original piece or not since it's not really my style, but I like it. Who knew they could do more than ride skateboards? Everyone keeps surprising me these days. I've got to stop judging people; I'm totally missing out on who they really are. During a break, Kate goes over and tries her hand at the drums.

Chad gives me a head bob as he sets his guitar on the stand.

"Hey."

"Hey," I answer back. "You guys sound fantastic."

"Thanks. So . . . you and Jake. Epic."

"Huh?"

"He posted a photo of you online."

"Oh." Oh, gosh. How many people follow Jake Taylor? That's overwhelming to think about.

"I mean, it looks like you, up at the mine?"

"Oh, yeah." I was hoping he'd send the photos to me. I didn't realize the whole world would view them as well.

"That's fly. He's chill."

"Okay." I mean, what do you say to that? You're chill too? If Kate's going to be going out with Chad, I'd better learn some skater lingo.

After our little chat, Chad makes a beeline over to Kate. She's still sitting at the drums awkwardly holding the drumsticks. Her face lights up as he approaches. He settles in behind her, takes her hands, and moves them to the different drums and cymbals. Together they bang out a cool rhythm. I snap a picture of the sweet moment. She can thank me later.

On the drive back to my house, Kate can't get the stupid grin off her face.

"Chad, huh?"

"He's really nice. And the band's good, right?" she asks.

"Yes, they are."

"Don't you think they should play a few songs at the Snow Ball?"

"Are you their agent now?"

"Don't give me a hard time or I'll start pressing you about Jake again."

"Fine. I noticed Chad couldn't take his eyes off of you. He totally missed his big riff because he was watching you."

"Really? I'm not sure if he likes me, though."

"Guys are hard to figure out." I can't believe I've stooped to quoting my mother.

"Jake and Chad are friends. Maybe we could double date," she says excitedly.

"You're getting ahead of yourself."

Kate drops me off. I'm glad everything is out in the open with her. Everything except the library tunnels, that is. And the Snow Ball. I hate keeping things from her.

I sprint up the stairs to check my computer and check out the photo Chad mentioned. It's not hard to find. The picture is of me sitting on a rock with the massive wooden door of the mine in the background. He hasn't labeled it or tagged me, which is probably a good thing. I stare at the photo for awhile, wishing there was one with the two of us together.

※

The week is interminably long and I'm anxious to see Jake and how he acts. Unfortunately, he doesn't send any more messages and I can't get my nerve up to text him again. I keep telling myself not to get all paranoid. He's probably just busy training. After a week away, I pray he won't change his mind.

In an attempt to fill my time and keep myself from going crazy, I decide to take Big Jim's advice and find a local story to investigate. It's going to be hard to do here in Silver Springs—the most boring town in existence. Then I think about the recent slew of deceased animals—the fish at the creek, the bird Duchess carried home and her mystery illness, the squirrels at the mine. Environmental stories are always good. Everyone wants a healthy planet and a safe place to live. Maybe there's some contamination at the mine I can discover.

Armed with one of Dad's hospital masks, little plastic containers, insulated rubber cleaning gloves, a shoe box, some labels, and plenty of hand sanitizer, I head off to investigate. I spend the afternoon driving and hiking around Silver Springs to gather soil from the various entrances of the mine and water samples from the stream and pond. In an attempt to be thorough I take plenty of photos and notes. I even find a decaying bunny. Score! Using a stick I push the disgusting thing into the box.

My dad, excited about my idea—probably because it doesn't have anything to do with boys—helps me send all the items off to a friend of his at a Denver lab. Now all I have to do is wait.

Chapter 11

Jake

I shoot down to the halfpipe. Picking up speed, I fly up the side, look toward the crowd, and see Sophie. She waves, then starts playing the tuba. What? I pull my eyes open and shake the stupid dream from my head. Slowly I realize the loud bellowing noise is continuing even though I'm awake. What is that?

No way I can go back to sleep now. I force myself out of bed, aching from the last few days. As I get dressed, I grimace at the multitude of bruises. Slowly, I make my way downstairs and find my parents at the kitchen table. Mom and I returned late last night from the condo.

"Morning, Jake. Did you hear the bugling this morning?" Mom asks as she sips her morning coffee.

"How could I miss it? What was that?" I ask while I grab a bagel.

"Apparently it was an elk," Dad explains. "I ran into our neighbor, Mrs. Maddox, at the market the other day and she warned me the bugling would start soon. The bull elk is searching for a mate."

"Couldn't he do it later in the day?" I grumble.

"You can't stand in the way when dealing with affairs of the heart. Maybe you should take some lessons from the forest crooner," he suggests.

"Sure, Dad. I'll start practicing my bugling. I'm sure that will impress the girls."

"Or, hopefully, at least Sophie Metcalf," he adds with a grin as my mother slaps his arm.

While we were up in the mountains, my mom invited the team over for dinner. We all squeezed into the small condo and Tommy and Dan, at the group's request, did an encore performance of the Jake and Sophie show. Not surprised she shared the info with Dad.

"What are you going to do today?" Mom asks, trying to get back on my good side. "It's Friday and all the other kids will be in school."

"Who knows. Veg? Recover?"

"Bill called yesterday," Dad says, changing the subject.

Now what? My week was awful. The last three days were a disaster. I don't know what happened. And to think, I had been so freakin' excited to start training again. Sunday was awesome, but it went downhill from there. I stupidly thought it would be like before, just throwin' down tricks, chillin' with friends, and trying some new moves. But no, it's a whole new ballgame now that I won the silver medal.

Now my agent's hounding me about something. Just what I need.

"He said one of your sponsors is planning a big advertising campaign around you to coincide with your next competition. If you medal they'll donate to your favorite charity, the Special Olympics. But Bill's worried about the whole thing after watching that television report on your training this week."

"I'd like to see him try the 1260. He couldn't even make one rotation, let alone three and a half," I snap.

"A lot of people expect you to continue to soar."

"I don't care what they expect!"

"Don't be too hard on him, honey. It was a tough week," my mom says.

"Jake, I'm just saying life isn't easy. You'll always have responsibilities and commitments."

"Dad, I'm sixteen not forty. Give me a break." I storm out the door.

Before the Olympics, there were no expectations. Now suddenly the pressure is on. Everyone is counting on me for something—my parents, my teachers, my sponsors, my coach, the press, my fans, now the Special Olympics.

I jump in the jeep and drive toward the mine. Sophie told me the hiking trail up the hill was difficult. Well, that's just what I need right now to clear my head and loosen my sore muscles. I park alongside the road, near the 4-wheel trail, then search for the path. It takes a while to locate. Judging from how overgrown it is, I'd say it's pretty obvious not many people use the trail. It's steep, going almost straight up the mountain, but that's what I need today.

As I climb the mountain I think about that McTwist 1260. Coach wants to further trick out my 1260 by adding a full flip to all the spins. I kept trying to nail the thing but could never get the last rotation in. The cameras were there on Tuesday to do a feature on me. They captured every fall, slip, and crash.

After each attempt I watched everyone's faces. The looks of anticipation and excitement changed to disappointment and skepticism. The reporter raised his eyebrows and jotted down notes. Tommy and Rachael kept glancing at each other. The worst was when Coach stopped yelling, shook his head, and averted his eyes.

I was terrible. The guys tried to act like it was no big deal. They said things like, "Hey, good warm up," and, "It's always hard to get back into it." What else were they going to say?

That night I tuned in to watch the report. The anchor and reporter sat in their comfy chairs in their air-conditioned studio, analyzing me. Questioning if I really had the stuff or if I was a sports one-hit wonder.

"Brent, thanks for your report. Some athletes fly onto the scene, then can't handle the big leagues."

"You're right. Jake Taylor gave us quite a ride, but maybe he doesn't have it in him to take it to the next level."

"Jake," my mom said, turning down the volume, "stop watching that. Don't let them get to you. Everyone has a bad day, especially since you were trying a new trick. Tomorrow will be better."

But tomorrow wasn't better. The next two days, training was something it had never been before. Frustrating. The fun was gone. I struggled to hit anything. Why can't it be like before when I was a nobody? When I did it because I loved it?

As I continue up Mount Thompson my sore muscles ache and my lungs burn but I keep pushing myself. I want to feel the pain. I need to feel it. As my exhaustion grows, the anger inside me finally begins to decrease. Out of breath, I make it to the top of the trail. Finding a large rock near the mine entrance, I sit and stare out at the valley.

What am I going to do? What if I did lose "it" and the silver medal was some fluke? If I don't have snowboarding what do I have? Nothing. I have nothing.

As I chuck stones off the mountain, I think about the 1260. I know I can get that trick. But there's so much attention focused on me now it's hard to get in the zone. I hate it.

People think I have such an amazing life. Well, it doesn't feel so amazing at the moment. What would it be like to be a regular high school kid down the hill getting ready for tonight's football game, his biggest worry being what he's going to do all weekend? Is that what I want? To quit snowboarding and be like everyone else?

No. Then, what do I want?

I want to snowboard on my terms. Not everyone else's. To do it for myself, because I like it. I want people to back off. I could always just snowboard as a hobby, but I don't want that. I want to compete. Unfortunately, that means being judged. Somehow I'll have to find a way to deal with that. I just don't know how.

Finally having cooled off some, I hike back down. My temper now mostly under control, I pay more attention to the shaded path this time. Fallen trees, starting to decay, lay across the trail making it difficult to pass. Huge mossy rocks scatter the area.

As I exit the trail, the sight in front of me makes my anger return; I want to punch something but there's nothing around to take the brunt. My jeep sits there like a wounded animal, all four tires flat. As I get closer I see they've all been slashed. Can this day get any worse?

Tucked under my windshield wiper is a note.

Keep your nose out of our business.

What the . . .?

I call home to break the news to my parents. As I wait, I try to calm down with little success. Why is the world against me?

Twenty minutes later, my parents show up with both cars. The sheriff and a tow truck pull up behind them. They all climb out of their vehicles and stand around staring at the jeep.

"What were you doing here, Jake?" asks Sheriff Miller.

"Hiking to the mine."

"Did you see anyone?"

"No."

"Jake, what if you had come down when they were doing this? You could have been hurt," says my mom.

"I'm fine, Mom"

"Wow, this is a new one for me," says the sheriff, scratching his head.

"I've never seen anything like it," agrees the tow truck driver. "Things like this don't happen here in Silver Springs."

Of course not. Only to me.

"Do you think he's safe?" asks my worried mother.

"Let's see the note," says Sheriff Miller. After I hand it over, he examines it, then says, "Do you have any idea what it means?"

"No, I've been out of town for most of the last two weeks. I've hardly seen anyone from around here."

"Did you cut anyone off?" asks my dad.

"No, Dad. I told you I didn't see anyone."

"Well, you obviously made someone mad."

"Thanks for the vote of confidence."

"I'm only saying people don't go around slashing tires."

"Your dad has a point," says Sheriff Miller. "There may be some anti-Jake people in town. Then again, it could be some hikers passing through causing trouble. Once in awhile we get those hippie types drifting from one place to the next. That note makes me think someone was messing with you. I don't think you have anything to worry about. Listen, I'm leaving town for a few days to see the grandkids. I'll be back Tuesday afternoon. But I'll have Deputy Grady keep patrolling the area."

As we fill out a report, my jeep is loaded onto the truck. Feeling defeated, I watch my damaged vehicle slowly being driven away.

Dad leaves to go back home and call the insurance company. Sheriff Miller heads back to the station. Mom and I drive into town to waste time while the tires are replaced. She suggests we go to Nora's Café to have some lunch while we wait. I agree, even though I don't have any appetite.

All eyes are on us as we enter the restaurant and sit at the counter. Can't anyone around here mind their own business?

Deputy Grady sits in the corner of the restaurant watching me while he eats a slice of pie. What's his problem? If he were out doing his job instead of stuffing his face, none of this would have happened.

We order some sandwiches then sit in silence, my mom unusually quiet. I'm sure she senses my mood and is afraid to set me off again.

"Hi, Jake." I look up to see Mallory, playing with her hair.

"Hey. What are you doing here?" I say, not doing a very good job of being friendly.

"We had a half day because of some teacher meeting. I saw your car being towed into town. Everything okay?"

"Yeah, just a little trouble."

"It better get fixed soon. I want you to take me on a ride."

As usual, she makes the conversation about her. The only things she ever talks about are herself or my fame. I'm not in the mood.

"See ya, Mallory," I say and turn back to my lunch.

She pauses, then walks away.

"Who was that?" asks my mom, carefully.

"Mallory."

"I gathered that. You were a little rude to her," Mom continues. "She's obviously interested in you."

"She's like everyone else—she wants something from me."

Out of the corner of my eye I see my mom staring at me.

"Jake, I don't like seeing you this stressed. You're putting too much pressure on yourself," she says.

"I'm not the one amping up the expectation level."

"Do you want to talk about it?"

"No." What good would that do? She doesn't understand. No one does.

The bell on the front door rings. Anxious to get away from my mom's concerned look, I turn to see who's entering. I watch as the one person who could improve my mood enters the restaurant. Sophie's radiant smile and effortless beauty fill the room with energy. Electricity surges through my veins. Oh man, I'm hooked.

Chapter 12

Sophie

"Valerie, Sophie. My favorite mother-daughter duo," Nora says as Mom and I walk into the restaurant.

"Hi, Nora," I say.

"How's everything these days?" Mom asks her.

"Good. You know, this Neighbors Helping Neighbors program is working so well I got my inventory done in half the time this month. A few of us retail shop owners decided to help each other out with the mundane tasks. It never seems like work when you're laughing with friends. Why didn't someone think of this years ago?"

"I know. Lee was right. It has helped all the businesses on the street create unity by increasing the community feel, while reducing our workload at the same time."

"I gave him a free piece of pie today to show my appreciation. Take the open table by the window so you can enjoy the beautiful fall day. I'll get your usual lunches started."

"So, is there a reason you asked me to lunch instead of going out with Kate?" Mom asks as we sit down.

"Can't I enjoy lunch with my mom when I have a half day of school?"

She looks at me with raised eyebrows as if to say "yeah, right."

"Okay, fine. She's at an orthodontist appointment. But we're going down to the mall in Denver tonight and I need some money."

"What happened to all your babysitting funds?"

"I don't have much left after paying my car insurance."

"You could get a job."

"I know. But there aren't many employment opportunities around here. And I don't want to charge for my tutoring—I like helping the kids. Besides, don't you and Dad want me to focus on my studies?" I ask innocently.

"Okay," she laughs. "Well, look who else is here."

I glance up and follow her gaze to the counter. There on a stool, turned completely around and leaning against the counter watching us is Jake. He's back! At seeing him, my heart does that little calisthenics routine that occurs every time I'm in close proximity to him. He's in jeans and a T-shirt. His arms are crossed against his chest, showing off those biceps that sweep me off my feet in my dreams.

He suddenly gets up and starts to walk over to our table. His mom, who was sitting next to him, follows along.

My mom stands up and shakes hands with Mrs. Taylor.

Okay, totally awkward.

As introductions are made I rack my brain to think of something to say. Come on, Sophie. Get your head in the game.

"When did you get back in town?" is the best I can come up with.

"Last night," he answers.

"We're having some lunch while we wait for his jeep to get fixed," his mom says.

"Why, what happened?" my mom asks.

Mrs. Taylor glances over at Jake. He ignores her so she answers, "He parked it by the trailhead to the mine this morning. When he got back from his hike his tires had been slashed."

Whoa. "You're kidding," I say, searching his face for answers.

"I wish," Jake responds, his tone strained, not at all the relaxed cavalier way he usually speaks.

"That's horrible," my mom says. "I can't believe someone around here would do such a thing."

"The sheriff thinks it was some hikers causing trouble," answers Mrs. Taylor.

"That's strange. Why don't you join us?" my mom asks indicating my chair.

"Thanks, Valerie."

Our mothers click immediately and sit down at the table, heavy in conversation. With them completely oblivious to us, Jake puts his hand on my elbow and leads me back to the counter where he had been sitting. Nora gives me a sideways look and a thumbs-up as she delivers my sandwich. Can she *be* any more obvious?

"I'm glad you're back. Life around here is incredibly boring without you."

"I didn't scare you off after asking you to the Snow Ball?"

"Hardly," I blush. Is he kidding? That's all I've been thinking about for five days.

"I still might. You haven't seen me dance yet."

I don't think there's anything he could do to scare me off now that I've seen a glimpse of the real Jake Taylor.

He cocks his head toward the table by the window where our mothers are busy talking. My mom's probably inviting Mrs. Taylor to be a part of Neighbors Helping Neighbors or something. "They sure hit it off," he says with a slight laugh.

"It's hard to find someone my mom can't chat with," I reply. Conversations come easily to her. I, on the other hand, always seem to stumble around in awkward silences. Or—when around Jake—talk way too much. "Your mom seems really nice," I add.

"Yeah, she's cool. She does a lot for me. Don't tell her I said that though."

"I bet she's upset about your tires. I can't believe they were slashed," I say, still shocked by the recent news.

"Yeah." His face darkens, the happy mood evaporating. Way to go, Sophie.

"Are you okay?"

"Not really, the last few days have been awful," he answers, his shoulders slumping.

"Why?"

"Didn't you tune into any sports channels this week?"

"No. Not really my thing, sorry. I thought you'd be in heaven up on the mountain, just you and your snowboard."

"So did I. But it didn't work out that well." He looks over to the corner of the restaurant. "What's wrong with that guy?"

I look over to see the deputy watching us.

"Deputy Grady?"

"I swear he has it in for me. He's been staring at me since we got here."

"Probably because you drive like a maniac. He's got to keep an eye on any public nuisance," I tease, trying to lighten the mood.

"No, I'm serious. There's something wrong with that dude."

"He was fine until you moved to town. Maybe he's not under your Jake Taylor spell."

He turns and grins at me. "Are you?"

"I'm getting there," I say, in an attempt to flirt. "Seriously, Deputy Grady's not that bad. In fact, he gave me some maps of other 4-wheel trails for us to explore."

"Really? Maybe we can go check them out sometime."

"I'd love to."

"How about this afternoon?"

"Shoot. I have plans with Kate tonight." I briefly debate canceling out on her. I don't want to lose a chance to spend time with Jake.

"That's okay. I'm exhausted anyway. How about tomorrow? I'll pick you up around noon?"

"It's a date."

I smile. It's a date. How am I ever going to be able to wait until tomorrow? With impeccable timing his mom walks up to us.

"Jake, sorry to interrupt. The mechanic called. They're done. It was very nice to meet you, Sophie. I hope to see you again soon."

"Thanks, Mrs. Taylor. Nice to meet you, too."

She pays for their lunch, then walks toward the door.

"Your mom looks lonely sitting all by herself, Bloomers," Jake says as he walks away. Oh yeah, I forgot all about her.

✳

Kate swings by in the afternoon to pick me up and we head out of town, down the mountain toward Denver.

"There's that stupid deputy again," Kate says as we pull onto the highway. The flashing lights are to the left as we turn right. "He spends so much time there that he may as well set up a souvenir stand. He could make some extra money."

"He obviously has no life. Pulling over trucks is the high point of his day."

"Maybe he's lonely. It's his way to meet people. Maybe if we play matchmaker and set Deputy Grady up with someone he'll stop giving so many tickets."

"And if he's busy with a girlfriend maybe Jake would stop thinking that the deputy's out to get him."

"Jake?"

"Oh, didn't I mention Mom and I ran into him and his mom at Nora's this afternoon?" I try to sound innocent, but can't control the huge smile on my face.

"These darn braces make me miss all the fun."

"It was totally mortifying, though. Our moms are like BFFs now." I then tell her about Jake's jeep.

"Geez. No wonder he's paranoid."

"I know, completely bizarre."

"Think someone targeted him?"

"Doubt it. Everyone loves Jake."

"Including you, now."

"So, what are we getting at the mall?" I say, ignoring her remark.

"Dresses for the Snow Ball, of course," she states.

"Don't we usually just raid each other's closet?"

"This year we may have dates. We need to look good."

"Dates?" Little does she know I really do have one. But I'm afraid to tell her, superstitious that talking about Jake and me will ruin everything.

"It's a possibility. We've gotta be ready."

My pulse suddenly rushes as I picture myself going to the dance with Jake. I can't even imagine walking into the crowded gym with him. I mean, it would be beyond amazing.

"Don't talk about it. You're gonna jinx everything," I say. Besides, I know there's a possibility I may not even be able to go with Jake. He warned me he'll soon be training and may not be in town for the big night. No matter what, it'll be fun to dress up. And if he's around, I'll look awesome and enjoy the most incredible night of my life.

❄

Saturday at noon Jake pulls up to my house. Before he can come up to the door, I hurry out to meet him and climb into the jeep.

I've been waiting for hours, while questions have kept running through my head. What am I going to wear? What are we going to talk about? How should I act? I tried to tell myself it was no big deal, but I couldn't make myself believe it. Sure, we've been alone before, but this is different. Those weren't planned—just random circumstances that threw us together. This could possibly—maybe, hopefully—be the start of something.

"Hi," I say, realizing I'm probably acting way too eager.

God, help me be myself today.

"Hey. Where to? Should we try one of those new trails?"

"Sure, I brought the printout Deputy Grady gave me. I see you got new tires."

"Yeah, all better."

"I still don't get it; why would someone do that?"

"I don't know. I keep thinking about the note, but I don't know what it means."

"You didn't tell me about a note."

"It said, 'Keep your nose out of our business.'"

"Maybe we should retrace your steps and see if we can figure it out."

"I know you like mysteries, but I really don't think we'll find anything."

"Aren't you curious?"

"I guess so. You really want to spend the day looking into this?"

"Why not?" I don't care what we do as long as we do it together.

"Okay, back to the mine we go."

We drive over to the mine road. Jake doesn't want to risk parking along the road again, so he pulls onto the 4x4 trail and parks along the edge. We walk back to the hiking path and start up.

"Did you see anyone yesterday when you were here?" I question.

"No, no one, Detective Sophie."

I ignore his teasing. "Did you hear any strange sounds?"

"Besides the amorous elk? No."

"Anything out of the ordinary?"

"To tell you the truth, I was really angry and didn't pay any attention to my surroundings."

"Oh." I forgot . . . he said it had been an awful week. I guess he meant it. "I thought training again would make you feel like the blasting sticks used to make the mine," I say, hoping to lighten his mood.

"Dynamite?" he shakes his head. "No, you should see me with my shirt off."

I blush at the thought.

"I look like advanced and intermediate ski runs," he explains.

"Black and blue?"

"Yeah," he looks down at his feet. "But that's the least of my problems."

"Was training *that* bad? Do you want to talk about it?"

He looks at me, then sighs. "After I saw you on Sunday—which was great—things began to fall apart. I was trying this new trick and couldn't get it. There was some sports show there and they taped the whole thing. They reported that I've lost my edge and then questioned my abilities."

"Really?" I can't imagine having my failings broadcast to millions of people.

"The rest of the week I couldn't hit anything either. I feel like everyone—my coach, my team, my sponsors, the press, my fans—is expecting too much from me. To top it off, my agent called yesterday to hassle me."

I try to think of some way to encourage him but can't relate at all to the pressure he must be under.

"Can you talk to Rachael? You mentioned she's been through a lot. Did she ever have to deal with something like this?"

"No. Rachael had other issues." He tells me the tragic story of Rachael's friend, Emma, and the bad decisions she made which, in the end, took her life.

"Oh, that's horrible."

"Yeah, I guess one good thing came out of her example: the rest of us learned from her mistake."

"What about Tommy? Would he understand?"

"Tommy's a free spirit. Even though he's one of the best, he's much 'wilder,' so he doesn't have all the pressure from sponsors. Maybe he has the right idea. It sure would be a lot more fun to just do your own thing."

"I wish I could help you." If only I could solve the mystery of who messed up his car and at least help with one of his problems.

"You are, by being here with me," he says, smiling at me.

I'm totally out of breath as we exit the shaded hiking trail near the mine entrance. Jake looks completely unfazed after the strenuous hike.

"Looks the same to me," Jake says as we walk around the area.

"Well, someone's been here recently," I say.

"How do you know?"

"I was here a few days ago and that wasn't there," I point to some crumpled beer cans and cigarette butts by the mine.

"You have a keen eye, Detective Sophie. I guess that would support Sheriff Miller's theory of hikers just causing trouble. But I never saw anyone; I just sat over there and threw rocks."

"Threw rocks? Maybe you accidentally hit someone."

"Maybe I should find another way to vent."

"Yeah, don't take it out on poor innocent rocks," I tease.

He grins but still looks miserable. I rack my brain trying to think of a way to help him, when a discussion I had with my youth leader pops into my head. *Thanks, God.*

"Umm . . . I hope I don't sound like I'm preaching, but it seems to me that God gave you a really special talent, Jake. My youth group leader told me that it's our job to try and figure out how to use our gifts to glorify God. Rather than focusing on how rough things are for now, maybe you could think about how God wants you to use your skills."

"How could snowboarding ever help anyone?" he asks doubtfully.

"It might sound odd, but your ability brought you to the attention of lots of people. Think about all those kids who look up to you. You can influence them and the choices they make."

"Hmm, I've never thought about it like that before."

He doesn't seem to think I'm totally ridiculous, so I continue. "Remember when I told you that when I have problems I go to my rock by the Claim Jumpers creek? What I usually do is pray, then listen for God to speak to me. God's specialty is cleaning up our messes. We've just got to stop trying to do everything on our own."

"God *answers* you?" he asks, a tiny hint of amusement in his voice.

"Sure, sometimes it's that little voice inside that guides me. You know, those little thoughts that pop into your head. He's usually telling me to stop trying to solve it by myself. Obviously, I still need a little help with that. Or sometimes he'll bring people into my life to help me grow into the person he wants me to be."

"So God could have sent me you?" he asks.

I blush. Could I really be an instrument God is using? Wow, I never thought about that before. I guess you never know who you might influence. And to think, if I hadn't gone out of my comfort zone and stayed with Jake and his team that day, I never would have seen a different side of him or felt comfortable enough to tell him these things.

"All I know is if you rely on God, he'll always lead you down the right path. He has a special plan for you, just let him guide you to it. And maybe next time you should try hurling prayers instead of rocks," I say as I elbow him and hope I didn't just scare him off. But if I did, I guess he's not the one for me.

"I'll think about it, Bloomers. You know, I've never met anyone like you." He smiles, then reaches over and takes my hand. A chill runs through me. Yay! I guess being all church-y didn't scare him away. . . . *Thank you, Jesus!*

"Did you and Kate have fun on your girls' night out?" he asks as we head back down the trail.

"Yeah, we went to the mall," I answer, though it's hard to concentrate since all I can focus on is the warmth of his hand. I decide not to tell him about the new dress I bought. Since he told me his crazy schedule may keep him from going to the dance, I don't want him to feel bad if we end up not going together. He has enough pressure without me adding to it.

"You didn't go to the football game?" asks Jake.

"No way. Our quarterback has been out with the flu. I'm sure it wasn't much of a game."

"I guess I'm behind on my Silver Springs gossip, having been gone all week."

"Well, here's a juicy item. Chad and Kate have something going on."

"Really? That's cool. Chad's a good guy."

"Yeah, they're cute together."

He stops at a large boulder and leans his back against it. He takes my other hand and our fingers intertwine. Sunlight filters through the trees. . . . Could this be any more ideal?

"You think they're speculating about us?" he asks with a grin.

"Most likely . . . that's how small towns work."

"Does it bother you if people talk about us?" he asks, pulling me closer to him.

"No." I smile back, trying to ignore my increased heartbeat.

I think he's about to kiss me, when—my phone starts to moo. Yes, moo.

Romantic moment broken.

The twerp's dead. He's totally ruining my almost love life.

"Know anyone who wants a ten-year-old brother? I'd be willing to sell mine for cheap."

Jake laughs and drops my hands while I check my phone.

"It's a reminder. I promised Sam I'd play soccer with him this afternoon. He must have entered it into my calendar."

"The kid's good with cell phones."

"You have no idea."

"Well, let's not keep him waiting," Jake says and leads me the rest of the way down the trail.

"We never figured out who slashed your tires or left the note."

"Oh well. Maybe the sheriff was right and it was a random incident."

We drive back through town toward my house. Sam sits on the front steps, his soccer ball in his lap as he waits for me. Everest lies at his feet. As we pull up Sam's eyes bulge out.

"Hey, buddy," Jake says to him as we climb out.

Sam stares at Jake. For once my brother is speechless.

"I hear you and Sophie are going to play soccer. Can I join you?"

"Okay." It cracks me up to see Sam this still and silent.

"Are you sure you're up for the challenge?" I ask Jake.

"I think I can handle it."

"You may have a silver medal, but I was the top scorer on my second grade team."

"Consider me warned. Game on."

Sam looks at us nervously, but he warms up as the three of us kick the ball around the front yard. Everest runs between our legs, trying to be part of the action. Jake shows off some fancy footwork, then teaches the moves to a fascinated Sam. As the afternoon light starts to fade, Jake heads toward his car.

"Thanks for playing with us, Jake," says Sam.

"Sure, any time. See ya later," he says to Sam. He looks at me and winks, then climbs in his jeep and, shifting into gear, takes off.

This hidden Jake that most people don't see is amazing. I watch him drive away, while my heartbeat slowly returns to normal.

Chapter 13

Jake

The image in my side mirror cracks me up. Sophie is standing in the middle of her front lawn watching me drive away, while Sam and Everest run circles around her. What is it about her that always puts me in a better mood? Spending the day with her helped me forget about all the other stuff for awhile. Of course she's beautiful, but she's also easy to be with and probably the one person who doesn't expect something from me. She doesn't even seem to care about my celebrity status. If only our kiss hadn't been interrupted. Next time.

Glad all the anger and disappointment of the past week is gone for the moment, I crank my music and whip around the corner toward my house. Suddenly flashing lights fill my rearview mirror. Great. I pull over and Deputy Grady approaches.

"Yes, Deputy?"

"Going a little fast again, Jake."

"Sorry. I'll slow it down."

"I'm afraid I've given you too many warnings. License and registration."

"Oh, come on."

He stands there staring at me.

"Fine." I reach over and open the glove box. Things tumble out of the overcrowded compartment as I grab the registration.

"Out of the car."

"What?"

"Out of the car."

I give him a look, then push open the door and climb out. I lean against the hood and wonder why he's hassling me while he searches around inside. He picks something off the floor mat on the passenger side and holds it up.

"Want to explain this?" he says holding up a small bag.

"Never seen it before." Is that what I think it is?

"Do you know the penalty for the possession of marijuana by a minor?"

"Are you serious? It's not mine."

"That's what they all say."

"I'm serious! Besides being illegal, it's wrong and dangerous, and would completely ruin my snowboarding. I wouldn't touch them."

"Evidence doesn't lie, Jake."

"Whoever messed with my car yesterday must have planted it."

He searches the rest of the vehicle, then says, "Lucky for you, since this is your first offense and you have less than an ounce we can clear this up with a fine . . . this time. But I'll be watching you and if you're caught again the consequences will be greater. Probation, mandatory drug tests, or entering the juvie system probably wouldn't be too great for your career."

Despite my innocence, I feel sick.

"Let's call your folks," he says after he writes out a ticket.

"Is that part of the recommended penalty?"

"Watch your mouth. I'd say you're lucky."

"Yeah, well, I'm not feeling lucky."

※

By the time I pull into the circle drive, my parents are standing on the porch waiting for me.

"What is with you?" Dad asks through gritted teeth. "We raised you to know better than to do drugs. Marijuana today, what's next?"

"It wasn't mine."

"Oh really? And whose was it?"

"Probably whoever trashed my car."

"Why would they leave a half-smoked joint behind?"

"To mess with me."

"Jake," Mom says, "the sheriff went over the car yesterday before it was towed to the garage. He didn't find anything."

"Sophie and I went back there today to look around."

My parents stare at me then look at each other.

"Go inside. We'll talk in the morning," Dad huffs.

After a hot shower to clear my head, I hear their voices wafting up from the kitchen. I sneak back downstairs to listen.

"Do you believe him?" asks Dad.

"I want to, but I'm not sure," answers Mom. "You should have seen him with those girls in L.A. They were on something and he didn't seem surprised. They said he had promised to party with them."

"He knows better than that!"

"He's been exposed to a lot this past year. I don't know where his head's at. You've got to admit his grades and snow-boarding aren't what they used to be. And there's been a few times recently that he's snuck off to do who knows what."

"It's the pressure."

"That's what I thought, but what if we're wrong and he's in trouble?"

"You really think the pot was his?"

"I hope not, but what are the chances someone planted it in his car this afternoon? Something is going on with him. He's not acting like himself. Where do you think he could have gotten drugs?"

"Maybe he's involved with some low life-drug dealer. It could explain why his tires were slashed."

"How could we not know if that was going on?"

"I don't know."

"We really messed up," my mom says through tears. "We let him pursue his snowboarding passion and in the process pulled him from church, friends, and a grounded community."

"Marcy, we sacrificed a lot so we could always be together and give him a strong foundation. Maybe we could have tried harder to keep going to church, but we moved here to give him a wholesome environment. We've always told him that doing drugs is wrong because it would harm his body. We've tried our best to raise him with morals and family values," my dad counters.

"Some good it did. The fame is devouring him."

Having heard enough, I turn around and head back to my room. Anger surges through me, stunned they think I could be involved with drugs. I'm being set up and my own parents don't even believe me. Could things get any worse?

❄

I'd been up for hours already on Sunday, painstakingly going over every detail of my story and answering my parents' endless questions when the phone began ringing off the hook.

"How does everyone know about this already?" I ask when my mom hangs up after attempting to calm my agent down. Both he and Coach are completely freakin' over the news of my supposed drug use. Why do people believe the worst?

"I don't know," she says, shaking her head as we sit around the kitchen table, still in our pajamas, dealing with the unfolding situation. "Bill and your coach both said a call from an investigative reporter woke them up first thing this morning."

"Last night the deputy said it was just a ticket and fine, but it would be kept out of the press."

"Things like this never remain a secret," Dad states gloomily.

"It's only a matter of time before it's in the papers and all over the Internet," says Mom.

"I can't believe this," I grumble and slump in my chair. So much for my plans to be a positive role model for my fans and show them it can be cool to make good decisions.

"When things seem the most bleak we must have faith," encourages Mom. "We may have fallen away from attending Mass, but God is always faithful. He can get us through this."

"I hope so, because dealing with this is going to take a miracle."

Completely defeated, I head to my room. Why doesn't anyone believe me? If they knew me they'd know I wouldn't do drugs. Suddenly it feels like Kansas all over again—everyone turning their backs on me.

What am I going to do? I obviously can't handle this on my own. I need help. Maybe Mom and Sophie are right and I should turn to God. Sitting by the window in my room, I try. *Lord, I know it's been kind of a while, but I'm in over my head. Can you help me?*

When my cell phone rings I almost ignore it, afraid of more bad news, but I answer when I see it's Sophie.

"Hey."

"Hi. I hope I didn't wake you. Since you're in town, I thought I'd see if you'd like to go to church with us this evening and check out the youth Mass I told you about," she says cheerily.

"Don't think so. We're kinda dealing with some things this morning. But maybe you could pray for me while you're there. I could use the help."

"Sounds like you *should* come to church with me. What's going on?"

"After I left your house, Deputy Grady pulled me over for speeding and found marijuana in my glove box."

"Drugs?" I can hear the surprise and disapproval in her voice.

"Sophie, let me . . ."

"Wait. He thought it was yours? That's crazy!"

"You're the only one who seems to believe it wasn't mine."

"Of course I believe you. I know you wouldn't do that." Her unquestioning faith in me is amazing.

"And to make it worse, some reporter is already on the story."

"This is really serious. What are we going to do?"

"We?"

"We were the last two in the car. If it wasn't yours or mine, then someone put it there."

"But who?"

"I don't know, but whoever it is must want to bring you down. What's the fall-out so far?"

"The no-drug policy means my position on the team is in jeopardy. Even when the drug test they're insisting on comes back negative, the fact that I was in possession of it means they'll speculate about my intentions, especially after my pathetic performance. My agent said when the story breaks my sponsors may drop me. My parents don't believe me. And who knows how long till the scandal hits the media? In other words, I'm toast."

"Don't worry, Jake. We'll prove you're innocent. We just need a plan."

"Thanks for believing in me, Sophie. I actually was thinking of asking Deputy Grady how the story was leaked. It was supposed to have been kept quiet."

"Good idea. I know he's probably not your favorite person at the moment but, as others keep reminding me, he was only doing his job. I still think he likes us, so he'd be a good one to get on our side. Maybe he can help us figure this mess out."

"I highly doubt it. He's never been a fan, but I've got to try something."

"Can we meet this afternoon to figure out our next move?"

"Sure, somewhere away from town though. I'm not in the mood to face anyone."

"Okay. Why don't we go to the other side of the mine, to the ore crushing mill? No one ever goes there. We'll be totally alone. I can get away around two."

"Alright. See you this afternoon," I say, then hang up.

After our long talk this morning my parents seem to be willing to give me the benefit of the doubt. I persuade them I have no intention of making things worse and promise to keep a low profile, so they reluctantly agree to let me stay behind while they head to Denver for a pow-wow with our lawyer. I assure myself my plan to track down Deputy Grady totally falls within these parameters. After all, talking to him can only help, and I'm taking my mom's SUV to ensure no one in town will see me driving around.

I drive toward Main Street and park on a side road to avoid being seen. As I walk toward the boardwalk, I spot him about a block down at the rear entrance of the sheriff station. He's leaning against his squad car with his back toward me, talking on the phone.

I slowly approach, hoping he'll finish his conversation so I can get some real answers. As I get closer I can't help but hear his part of the conversation.

"You worry too much. I got things under control."

He kicks a rock as he listens.

"No. He's been neutralized," he says. "Anyway, I'll be there in a few minutes."

He shoves his phone in his pocket and turns around. He jumps a little when he sees me, then glances around.

"You really shouldn't eavesdrop," he says with a menacing look after he gains his composure.

This is not going as planned.

"Sorry. I didn't mean to surprise you."

"What are you doing here?"

"I wanted to talk with you for a minute."

"Make it quick. I have an appointment."

Great. Now I've ticked him off.

"I was wondering if you had any idea how the press found out about my ticket."

"Maybe one of your paparazzi was lurking and saw what happened."

"But I'm innocent. It must have been someone else's dope."

"Jake, don't blame others for what you've done."

"I was set up! Sophie was with me at the mine yesterday afternoon. We were looking around to see if we could figure out why someone slashed my tires. Whoever did that probably also planted the weed."

"Cool the whole amateur detective thing, Jake. All this snooping might get you into hotter water."

I look at him, not sure what he's getting at.

"If you're right and someone did set you up, aren't you risking a lot by involving Sophie?" he adds.

"What?"

"I mean it would be a shame if anything happened to her because she's hanging around a kid like you," he says coldly, then climbs into his squad car.

I must be losing it because that sounded an awful lot like a threat you'd hear in the movies. As I watch him pull away, I replay our conversation in my head. Somehow I screwed up. Why was he so furious when he saw me standing there? Suddenly I flash on a memory and realize I've seen his anger before. Whoa . . . the glaring man at the pizza place in Breckenridge—it was him!

Something's not right with that guy. With a growing bad feeling about the deputy and nothing else to do since I really don't want to go home yet, I decide to follow him.

He probably doesn't know Mom's SUV, but tailing someone in a small town is tricky. He meanders through town and out toward the highway. I feel totally conspicuous driving this slowly. Pick up the pace, man. But I stay back to avoid suspicion. He turns west on the highway and in a couple miles turns onto a small dirt road.

I have no idea where this goes and am not sure if I should follow. But I need to clear my name so I keep trailing him. The narrow dirt road winds through the trees as it climbs the mountain. I don't see his car and there are no side roads for him to turn off, so I slowly keep going. Eventually it levels off and I spot a clearing up ahead. His squad car is parked next to several trucks. One of the trucks I've seen before: the huge black pick-up with Texas plates and the skull and crossbones sticker in the window that blocked one of the side roads when I was first searching for the 4-wheeling road up to the mine.

This must be the old logging road at the top of the mine. I shift into reverse and back up, then swing into a break in the trees near a collapsed log cabin and park on the backside of the wooden building. Between the structure, the trees, and the black paint job, I hope the car is hidden.

As I climb out and slowly make my way through the woods toward the trucks, I question my sanity. What am I doing? I'm going to feel like a fool if he's just meeting some buddies. But whatever he's doing doesn't look like part of his job.

Stealthily moving over the twigs and pinecones, I try not to make any noise. Newly fallen Aspen leaves help pad the ground. As I approach, I see the path to the mine entrance about twenty feet below. Staying in the shadows of the trees, I inch closer. Urgent voices fill the quiet air and I strain to hear what they're saying.

From this angle I can't see the mine door but three men suddenly emerge like they were inside the mine, and Deputy Grady is one of them. He's a head shorter than the others. Some tall, greasy dude seems to be controlling the situation. The third is a huge body builder type.

"Are you sure the kid's not onto us?" asks greasy dude.

"I just saw him. He's clueless," answers Deputy Grady.

Kid? Does he mean me?

"I don't need to tell you what's at stake here. We don't need some smart-aleck kid blowing it for us."

"Don't worry," the deputy continues, "I'm sure he'll stay away now; he has his own problems to deal with."

"What about the girl?"

"She's only been up here with him. The folks from Silver Springs rarely come up here; that's what makes this place perfect. I just wasn't counting on the new kid in town being such a pain. But I'll keep an eye on her."

Sophie? Concern creeps over me. What's going on? I reach for my phone to record them, but I must have left it in the SUV.

"Let's just get rid of them," says Muscles.

"You're an idiot. They're probably too stupid to figure it out anyway. Besides, he's famous; if something happens to him the media will swarm the place and that would kill our little operation. But if they cause any more trouble I'll give you the go-ahead," says the greasy boss man.

The blood drains from my face. Are they really debating killing me? I half expect Tommy to come traipsing through the woods at any moment laughing that he punked me.

A fourth guy walks over to them. This one is covered in tattoos. But what really catches my eye is the semi-automatic weapon draped across his body. This is no joke. These dudes are crazy serious.

O Lord, what did I get myself into? What do these guys think I know?

"Don't worry, I've got it all under control," says Deputy Grady.

"Really? Those four slashed tires you left him didn't keep him away," says Mr. Muscles.

Despite the relatively warm day, my body instantly goes cold. I should have known Deputy Grady was the one who jacked up my jeep.

"What if the kid suspects something and goes to the sheriff?"

"Sheriff Miller trusts me completely. He'd never believe some pot-carrying kid over me. I'm his ticket to retirement. That snowboarder has no credibility now."

I always knew this guy was a jerk.

"It's gonna be fun watching him fall from glory," gloats Muscles.

"Yeah, all I had to do was plant some dope, place an anonymous phone call to the press, and he's history."

He set me up. But why?

Muscles goes back toward the mine and soon emerges carrying a wooden crate. What are they storing up in the mine?

Muscles carries the box up the hill toward me. Deputy Grady follows along.

Too scared to move, I lean back against the rough bark of a tree. Afraid even my breathing will give me away. This is no time for nerves. I've got to get out of here. I carefully make my way back to the SUV, staying deep in the woods. I catch my breath as the cruiser slowly passes down the dirt road. Luckily he doesn't even look my way as he drives by. I climb in the SUV and follow behind, keeping a safe distance between us. When I get close to the highway I pull to the side. Through the trees I can see his police car stopped along the side of the main road. I'm trapped for now. He'll see me if I leave.

Soon a large delivery van barrels down the highway through the canyon. Deputy Grady steps out of his car and waves the van over. It pulls up in front of his car; the flashing lights turn on. A routine speed trap? I'm about to exit the dirt road while he's distracted writing a ticket to the driver, when I notice a guy on the passenger side of the van get out and open the sliding van door. He scans the area, then walks over to the police car.

What the heck is going on?

He opens the back door of the cruiser and pulls out the large crate from the backseat. He carries the box to the van and places it in the back. He slides the door shut again and climbs back in the van.

Soon the van pulls away, followed by the squad car. My hands shaking, I hightail it out of there before I get caught.

Thankfully my parents are still out when I get back home. I debate whether to tell them everything I just saw but realize I don't know what I saw. My brain needs to process it all first.

Pacing around my room, I try to make sense of what I witnessed. What are those guys up to? Obviously they've stashed something in the abandoned mine. I'll give them credit; it's a perfect hiding spot. And who would think twice about a police car pulling over a vehicle? And if anyone noticed the transfer of goods, who would question a cop? Especially "helpful neighbor" Deputy Grady. But what could be in the crate? Must be something that was stored in the mine.

That day Sophie and I drove up to the mine we saw the deputy there. We must have surprised him. No wonder he gave us info about other trails. He wanted us to stay away from the place. But I screwed up their plan and went back. Probably freaked them out, causing the deputy to go all slasher crazy on my tires. When I ignored the subtle warning and went back there again they must have decided to destroy my credibility. Just like those hikers who also must have stumbled across the operation.

I think about the day I saw Deputy Grady at the pizza place in Breckenridge. He obviously wasn't happy to see me. I didn't recognize him in his street clothes, but now I'm positive it was him. What was he doing all the way in Breckenridge? Maybe he was making another delivery. But, of what?

Suddenly it hits me. Dad had read something about the resorts having a drug problem. No one could figure out the supply route. I think I just did.

Well, there's no way I'm going to sit back and let Deputy Grady get away with this. If I'm right and what he's hiding is drugs then that could really mess up a lot of people. I have to try and stop it. Too bad the sheriff's gone till Tuesday. Maybe

I should tell my parents, but it all sounds crazy and I'm not sure they'll take me seriously. I'll have to lay low till I can try to explain everything to Sheriff Miller.

Something I overheard continues to gnaw at me. They talked about keeping an eye on Sophie. A knot forms in the pit of my stomach at the thought of Sophie getting mixed up with these thugs. I can't let that happen. I need to protect her.

But how am I going to keep her at bay while I watch the deputy? She already plans to investigate. Even if I tell her to drop it, she's perceptive and will know something's up. Who am I kidding? There's no way she'll stay out of it. Somehow I've got to keep her safe. I can't risk anything happening to her.

I don't want to lose her, but her safety is the most important thing. Reluctantly, I realize the only way to protect her is to keep her far away from me until I can fix this mess.

How did everything fall apart? All I wanted was to find something to do around this stupid town and somehow I stumbled across a drug ring. I finally find someone I'm crazy about and now I have to cut her out of my life. My career is in total meltdown. On one side there's mounting pressure from everyone, and on the other, there's a group of thugs trying to destroy everything I've worked for. Before I can control myself, my anger spikes and my fist goes through the wall.

Chapter 14

Sophie

The drive up to the mill is another excellent 4-wheeling road, a steep incline with deep grooves and rocks. Since it's completely inappropriate for my little bug, I park near the trailhead and hike up the path.

Everest, whom I brought along, is oblivious to the seriousness of the meeting and thoroughly enjoys herself, sniffing at every mossy rock and tree as we walk.

Not seeing Jake, I let Everest loose to explore since she's practically choking herself pulling on the leash. The moment she's free, she bounds through the tall grass to chase a rabbit. At least, I hope it's a rabbit and not a skunk.

The northern exit of the mine is tucked into this side of the mountain. The heavy wooden beams of the door are almost totally covered by the trees and plants. I gingerly walk along the rails that connect the mine to the mill, using it as a balance beam, picturing how this all looked a century ago when it was still in use.

Everest's barks bring me back to reality and I watch her scamper to the other side of the ore crushing mill. I follow her trail around the rustic building that sits high on a rock, an ancient wooden ladder extending into the water.

Jake sits on a rock overlooking the creek, petting Everest. He glances up at me and smiles, but not the smile that makes his eyes sparkle and my heart skip a beat. He looks miserable. *Please, God, show me how to help him.*

"This place is cool, isn't it?" I ask as I sit next to him. "Long ago the stream had a much stronger flow and the miners used it for their ore-crushing operation. This meadow is actually where the mine workers stayed. If you search carefully you can find pieces of their bunkhouses. I'm not sure why they lived this far from town. Maybe they weren't respectable enough."

I hope he'll crack a smile, but he doesn't. Instead he just watches me. But not in the amused way he usually looks at me when I start rambling.

"We'll have to come again in the spring when the wildflowers are in full bloom. Columbines cover the field. Whoa, what happened to your hand?" I stare at the gashes on the knuckles of his right hand. "You didn't get in a fight with Deputy Grady, did you?"

"No, just my wall," he answers, gingerly flexing his hand.

"Ouch! Anyway, I've been thinking about what happened and have some ideas. I don't know if you got any answers from the deputy but, if not, we could call the reporter and ask how he found out about the story. Also, everything bad happens when you leave your jeep over by the mine road. Maybe we should park there again, set up a video camera, and watch what happens."

I smile at him expecting some reaction, but he continues to stare at his hand.

"Or, we could ask Sheriff Miller to dust the jeep for fingerprints. Also, what about taking a lie detector test to prove your innocence and clear your name?"

He sadly grins and shakes his head.

"I know you're down, but we can fight this. Don't give up."

He looks at me again, those beautiful blue eyes full of sadness and defeat. Then he reaches up and pushes a loose piece of hair behind my ear. The touch of his fingers against my cheek gives me a chill.

"Sophie, I don't think we should see each other anymore."

Whoa. Wasn't expecting that.

"If you're worried about involving me, don't be."

"No, I mean I don't want to see you anymore."

"Jake, don't try to protect me. Remember I'm tough, like Sally," I say, again trying to extract a smile.

"You don't understand."

"Yes I do. Things are bad at the moment, but you don't have to figure it out alone."

"Sophie, I mean it. I can't have anyone in my life right now."

"Jake, don't do this."

He closes his eyes and clenches his fist. "Listen, the only reason I've been hanging out with you was because of a bet with Chad."

"What are you talking about?"

"You were the only girl at school not interested in me. Chad bet me I couldn't get you to like me."

"What?!" I feel like I've been punched in the stomach.

"It wasn't a very hard challenge. But now I'm done. Don't need the distraction. I've got too much on my hands."

"Distraction? You're serious?"

"Yep."

I stare at him for a while, his words replaying in my mind. He keeps his eyes on the ground. Realizing he means it, I force myself to stand up.

"You self-absorbed pig. Well congratulations, you finally did it. You got your perfect blindside. Who would've guessed you'd accomplish it not on the slope but by backstabbing me?!"

I hook Everest to her leash and storm away. I hurry through the tall grasses trying to get out of there as fast as I can. But in my haste I stumble on one of the footings to the old bunkhouses. I curse the tears filling my eyes, making it hard to see where I'm going. I should never have trusted him. Why did I fall for his too-good-to-be-true looks and charm?

Halfway down the trail I think about the new outfit I purchased for the Snow Ball. Just yesterday I was excited about the stupid dance. Now I'd like to stuff a real snowball down Jake Taylor's throat. What an arrogant, slime-infested creep.

When I finally get home I'm relieved to find the rest of my family still away at Sam's scout picnic. Sometimes the people you love are not what you need. Like when you feel like a complete idiot. What was I thinking? I knew he was trouble. Why did I let myself fall for him?

I throw myself on the couch, ready to let the tears flow when I see his stupid face smiling up at me from the sports magazine on the coffee table. Are you kidding me? I rip the full-page photo out of the magazine and march up to my room. I tack it to my bulletin board, then take target practice with my dad's darts, aiming at that grin of his. I'm a bit off and pierce his chin, but with the next dart I hit him directly between the eyes. I don't stop until the photo is in shreds. Satisfied, I brush my hands.

The gratification of my vengeance quickly dies though. I slowly sink down on my bed and miserably curl up in a ball. I squeeze my eyes shut, ignore the tears that roll down my cheek, and wonder who I'm more mad at—Jake or myself?

❋

Monday morning—yuck. Mondays are bad enough but this particular one will really stink. How am I going to make it through the day when I feel like someone ripped out my heart and trampled all over it? Lucky for me, Kate is in her own little Chad world, too distracted to notice my mood, and Jake doesn't make an appearance at school. Maybe his parents sent him off to rehab.

After a miserable day of conjugating verbs in Spanish and learning about Napoleon and his complexes, I hope to hurry home and continue my life as a recluse. But I'm not quick enough and before I can make my escape, Kate traps me by my locker.

"Okay, Soph. What's with you today?"

"Nothing," I say and continue to walk down the hall.

"Did something happen with Jake? I never asked how your date on Saturday went. I'm sorry, I should have asked sooner."

I stop and turn toward her; might as well get this over with.

"Saturday was great, I thought. But yesterday he told me to get lost."

"What? What happened?"

"He explained that he was only going out with me to win a bet with Chad," I snap.

"You're kidding? That doesn't make sense."

"Yeah, well tell your boyfriend thanks."

"Chad's not my boyfriend and don't worry, I'll give him a piece of my mind. Why didn't you tell me sooner?"

"I didn't want to talk about it." I know who I should have talked to. Instead of crying my eyes out on my bed, I should have gone to my rock at Claim Jumpers Creek and prayed. Maybe this afternoon.

"Want to go somewhere and vent or gorge on chocolate or something?"

"No. I just want to go home."

"Okay," she says, giving me a hug.

I must admit I feel somewhat better now that Kate knows. At least I don't have to pretend in front of her anymore. When I walk into the house, I see a note propped up on the kitchen table for me.

Sophie—got a call from Gary at the lab in Denver. Tests back on water and soil. No contamination found. Still waiting on the rabbit's toxicology results. Dad.

I crumble up the note and throw it on the floor. Figures. No investigative story to help boost my career. Why can't something go my way for a change?

Sam is in the family room watching cartoons. I plop down next to him, ready for an afternoon of mindless drivel when my phone interrupts by playing the theme from Sam's favorite TV show. He springs up ready to bolt out of my reach, but I ignore the latest musical menace and answer it.

"Yeah?"

"Hey, it's me," Kate says cautiously. "Where are you?"

"Home."

"Have you checked out the newest edition of *Celeb Sightings*? It came in the mail today. I just got home and was glancing through it."

"You know I never look at the thing." As a joke, Kate gave me a subscription to the tabloid last year.

"Well, I think you should take a look at this issue."

"Kate, I'm not in the mood to see Jake wrapped around some starlet."

"Um, you seriously need to check out page two and then give me a call back."

I hang up and reluctantly go find the pile of mail on the front hallway table. I pull out the magazine and flip it open, bracing myself to see more photos of Jake on his L.A. trip. But the image on the page confuses me. I stare at the page trying to grasp what I'm looking at.

My eyes nearly pop out of my head when understanding washes over me. My hand flies to my mouth as I gasp. I bolt up the stairs to my room and slam the door shut. I open the magazine again and stare at the photos. One oversized image takes up most of the page. It's a picture of me. Me. In a magazine. It's the photo Jake took of me on the rock with the gold mine entrance in the background. The one he had posted online. Below it is a zoomed-in close-up of my face. With sunglasses on and my hair in a clip it doesn't immediately look like me, but it wouldn't be hard for anyone in town to figure it out.

The headline above the photo reads, "Is Mystery Beauty Behind Snowboarding Superstar's Slump?" I pore over the short blurb.

Halfpipe Hero's recent troubles worry the snowboarding world. Last week the Olympic Silver Medalist completely underperformed, causing sports analysts to question his sustainability. A concerned friend shared this photo with us, speculating the mystery girl is the reason Jake Taylor has fallen from grace. Could she be the one distracting him from his training?

I reread the overdramatic paragraph. I can't believe I'm in some tabloid that is distributed around the country—around the world, for all I know. Hopefully, no one in Silver Springs besides Kate reads this rag. What a mess. I don't even want to be associated with the jerk and now, if anyone sees this, the whole town will not only think we're together but that I'm responsible for his woes. Disgusted, I fling the stupid magazine into the corner.

Tuesday, I'm too embarrassed to face anyone. Every time I pass someone in the hall, I can't help but wonder if they saw the photos. Do they think we're a couple? Do they blame me for ruining Jake's career?

The morning is confrontation-free. But my luck doesn't hold out. As I plop down at the lunch table, Kate and Chad join me. I stare at her, hoping I can convey "Why'd you bring the enemy here?" with my eyes.

"Sophie, I chewed Chad out this morning and he didn't have any idea what I was talking about."

Likely story.

"So, you didn't have a bet with Jake that he couldn't get every girl in Silver Springs to like him? Including the one hold-out, me?"

"No comprendo," he says and shakes his head.

I'm not in the mood for Skater Boy's wit.

"Well, I hope whatever you bet him was worth it."

"No, that's jacked up. There was no bet," he says somewhat earnestly.

"Whatever," I say and leave the room. Like he's going to tell me the truth.

I wander the grounds of the school, eventually settling on a quiet spot under a tree. *Okay, God, sorry I didn't turn to you right away. Please help me figure out a way to keep myself busy. I don't want to keep moping around feeling sorry for myself. Or continue to drown my sorrows in chocolate ice cream. Help me trust that you are here with me.*

With my love life in shambles and the whole environmental contamination investigation a bust, I need something else to fill my time. Maybe now's the time to follow up on an idea I had to take my photos of Silver Springs and make them into note cards to sell at the gift shop. Maybe I'll focus on a few more sites, then make some sample cards.

When the bell rings signaling the end of lunch, I'm happy with my new plan. But my momentary lighter mood disappears when Mallory and her posse ambush me at my locker.

"Can I help you?" I ask, trying to throw some attitude into my voice and not succeeding.

"Are you proud of yourself, Sophie?" Mallory sneers. The expression on her flawless face is twisted in hatred.

"Is this going somewhere? I need to get to class."

"We saw the article in *Celeb Sightings* yesterday. You screwed up Jake's life," she says, jabbing a perfectly manicured finger at me.

"He doesn't need my help screwing up his life. He's doing that on his own."

"We're warning you to stay away from him."

"Don't worry. I have no plans to spend any time with him. He's all yours," I say, then push my way through the semicircle of cheerleaders. Those two really deserve each other.

After school I tell Kate that, as much fun as it sounds, I can't go check out the cup stacking team. Instead, I drive into town to buy some cardstock at the general store to prepare for my new mission. Pulling into a parking spot, I say a quick prayer I don't run into Jake the Snake.

Thankfully the store is nice and quiet and seemingly Jake-free. Mrs. Harper is busy sorting though her long list of prescriptions with the pharmacist. I walk toward the back wall which houses scrapbooking supplies. As I pass one of the aisles, I notice someone out of the corner of my eye. I glance over and nearly jump. Jake is standing at the end of the aisle, flashing his annoyingly perfect smile. Why is he here? Should I turn around and leave? No. Then it dawns on me he's standing still—too still. Feeling like a fool, I realize it's some life-size sunglasses display. He must be their spokesman.

Relieved, I turn back toward the paper aisle, then change my mind. A brilliant idea pops into my head and I walk down to his display and stare at the cardboard cut-out of him. I slip my hand into my purse and pull out a pen. A moustache and devil horns would look good on Mr. Taylor, I think. I lean in ready to give him a mini makeover, but my inner voice tells me to stop. *You're right, God. It's not the store's fault he tore out my heart and stomped all over it.* So as much as I'd like to, I can't go through with it. But I can't quite let it go either. My eyes land on a bin of stocking caps and scarves. I wrap the frilliest pink scarf around his neck, then take the most granny-looking hat and put it on Jake's flat head. I pull it down until it covers his whole face. There, that's better.

Proud of myself, I back up to admire my handiwork. Satisfied and ready to leave, I spin around and bump right into someone.

"Oh. Excuse me."

I look up to see Deputy Grady. His eyes go from me to the hat-covered display and back.

Busted. Why didn't I do the right thing and just walk away? Now I'll probably get a defacing property ticket or something.

"Trouble in paradise?" he asks instead.

"Oh, sorry. It's just he's such a jerk. Are you going to give me a lecture or something?"

"No. I'll let you go this time. I thought you two were a couple."

"Definitely not."

"Glad to hear it, Sophie. Guys like Jake Taylor are trouble. I'd hate to see you get mixed up in his problems."

"No worries there."

Before he changes his mind about letting my indiscretion slide, I quickly grab the supplies I need then hurry to check out.

As Mr. Wilkinson rings up my purchase, I glance at the newspaper on the counter. The headline, "Superstar Falls Out of Orbit and Crashes to Earth," causes me to gasp. Jake's photo accompanies the article. As much as I hate to admit it, Jake was right. The press seems ready to indict him without all the facts.

"Isn't that shocking? I really thought he was a nice young man," says Mr. Wilkinson.

"I guess he had us all fooled," I answer. Not sure how I feel about Jake's perfect life unraveling. As mad as I am at him, I can't help but feel a little bad that everything's falling apart. I know how much he loves to snowboard. But maybe he brought it all on himself.

"Are you prepared for the storm?"

"Storm?" I ask, not sure I heard him correctly.

"Haven't you heard? A big storm is supposed to blow through sometime tomorrow. Could get quite a bit of snow."

Snow? No, it can't snow! Not this on top of everything else. There's no way I'm ready for the Snow Ball. I need more time to recover. And I'm definitely not ready to face the whole town. I think of the beautiful dress I picked out for the dance and feel like crying. Oh, stupid teen romances. Adolescence stinks sometimes.

Dear God, I know it's a selfish request, but can you please make the weatherman wrong and stop the storm?

Chapter 15

Jake

I can't stop thinking about Sunday afternoon. I hate that I hurt Sophie—she's so amazing—but it was necessary. If she had put any of the plans she'd posed into action, it wouldn't have taken her long to figure out something was up, and I couldn't risk her getting involved in this mess. Deputy Grady and the guys at the mine are way too dangerous. Ironically, after telling her to basically get lost I realized how much I really like her. Obviously I knew I liked her since I couldn't stop thinking about her, but seeing the confusion and hurt in her eyes felt worse than I thought it would. Watching her try to act tough almost made me ditch the whole plan and pull her into my arms. But knowing what the deputy is up to has changed everything. It's no longer about me and my reputation. Now it's about doing what's right and getting drugs off the street. Hopefully after I fix this mess I can make it up to her.

The past two days have been ridiculously tense around the house. We're all waiting for the story to hit the news. I convinced my parents to let me skip school and study from home. Whenever I could, I'd leave for a run and keep an eye on the deputy. With the sheriff still away, Deputy Grady stayed in town popping into all the businesses along Main Street. I was able to observe the nice system he's created. He makes an appearance, checks if anyone needs anything, then takes advantage of the retailer's generosity—free slice of pizza, free ice cream, free coffee, free pie. Under the pretense of helpfulness he eats his way up and down the boardwalk. He's created the perfect cover for himself. Who would ever suspect the deputy who began Neighbors Helping Neighbors of trafficking drugs?

My parents have pretty much been holed up in the house since Sunday making tons of calls to deal with the situation. Even though I know they have doubts, to everyone else they proclaim my innocence.

Bill is completely worried. My sponsors love my clean-cut image, and allegations of drug use could ruin their entire ad campaigns. Coach is still trying to figure out his next move. Even though the drug test will come back negative, the possession charge is a major problem.

The one thing I have going for me is the fact someone tampered with my jeep. In fact, our lawyer wants the jeep to be searched thoroughly and all the evidence and the jeep to be fingerprinted. Like there's a chance anything will be found. But he's hoping to play up the incompetence of the local authorities.

Tuesday afternoon, the story finally hits the paper. Sick of being the victim, I march up to my room and call the sheriff.

"Sheriff Miller here."

"Hi, sir. This is Jake Taylor."

"Well, hi, Jake. I just got back from a long weekend so I don't have any more information about your jeep yet. But I heard you had some additional trouble while I was gone. You know, marijuana use can lead to harder drugs. And all drugs can ruin your life."

"The marijuana wasn't mine. I would never do drugs. I'm being set up."

"And who would do that?"

"Deputy Grady."

Silence.

"Why do you think that?" he finally asks.

"I kind of followed him on Sunday and saw him meet some guys up at the mine. I overheard him admit to slashing my tires and planting the joint. I think they're stashing drugs up there. Then the deputy pulls over a vehicle and hands over the stuff."

More silence.

"They're probably behind the problems at the resorts and that story about the hikers seeing those ghosts at the mine," I add.

"Jake, those are very serious accusations, and you must have misunderstood what was going on. I trust Deputy Grady completely. He's been working with the National Park Service to preserve the mine, and his job entails pulling over speeders."

"I know it sounds crazy, sir, but please believe me."

"Jake, I realize you're under an incredible amount of stress, and having your tires slashed would make anyone nervous. But lying about a law enforcement officer can make things a lot worse for you. Deputy Grady is a good officer. In fact, now that he's here I'm hoping to retire soon and spend more time with the grandkids."

"Sir, I'm not lying."

"Jake, I like you. But I'm warning you, son, you need to take responsibility for your actions and face the consequences."

"Can you at least watch him and see if he's doing anything suspicious?"

"I'll consider it, but I'm not making any promises," he sighs.

"Thanks."

Not sure why I thought it would be so easy. Thanks to Deputy Grady no one believes me. Sophie's words about how I acted arrogant when I first got to town bounce around in my head. Okay, maybe it's also because I put on too much of a carefree attitude. But now what? Do I call the feds? No, they'll contact the sheriff, who'll tell the deputy, who'll move the operation. My parents? Same scenario. Take the advice on the note and mind my own business? I think back to Rachael's friend and how drugs messed her up and in the end she died because of them. No, my conscience won't let me do that. If I can help get drugs off the slopes and streets, I've got to try; it's the right thing to do.

If I can get proof, the authorities will have to believe me. But how do I go about doing that? I need a plan. I need to get back up there without being detected to get the proof of their operation.

❄

Wednesday morning the phone doesn't stop ringing; probably journalists wanting a statement. I'm afraid they'll soon start camping out on the front lawn. If it weren't for caller ID, I'd probably have missed the call from Sheriff Miller.

"Jake, I talked with Deputy Grady. He's not sure what you thought you saw but as I told you, he's been working with Park Service to keep the mine in good condition. Frankly, we're concerned you'd make such a wild accusation to protect yourself. Lying will not get you out of this mess. Tell the truth, clean yourself up, and in time you might be able to get back to winning those competitions. One more thing, let your parents know I'll be there in awhile to thoroughly examine the jeep."

After I hang up I sit there, fear prickling up my spine. He told Deputy Grady my suspicions. Now Grady knows I'm onto him!

It's all up to me. No one else is going to help. If what I'm about to do doesn't work, not only is my life as a snowboarder over, my actual life may be over.

I wish I could call Sophie. But I did the right thing in protecting her. The danger just intensified, and if having her hate me keeps her safe, then that's a trade-off I'm willing to make. Because if anything happened to her I couldn't live with it.

I take off on foot toward the hiking trail to the mine. With my video camera in hand I push myself, making it up the mountain in record time. As I near the top, I hear the thugs talking. Moving as slowly as possible, I stay hidden among the thick trees, keenly aware the snap of a tree branch could alert them of my presence.

I peer down through the trees from above the mine, and the three men I'd seen the other day come into my line of sight. I don't see Deputy Grady anywhere. Muscles has traded in his semi-automatic for a rifle. Okay, we're dealing with multiple weapons here. The boss man stands away from the other two as he talks on his cell phone. I pull out the camcorder and start to record.

He stuffs the phone in his pocket and walks over to the others.

"Okay, we need to get ready to move everything. Things are getting too hot here. Better to move the operation than risk getting caught. The truck can't get back here for a few days, and a storm is on the way tomorrow. We'll leave Saturday," he tells the others.

"This place is perfect. Can't we just get rid of the kid and stay here?"

The blood drains from my face.

"I told you, he's too famous. We can't risk the huge investigation and media coverage that would come if something happened to him. Right now no one believes his story. But if he causes any more trouble, we may need to reevaluate and kill him anyway," he adds with an evil grin.

I shiver at their words, then carefully make a giant loop through the woods to get a shot of the front of the mine. Once in position I'm disappointed to see the mine door shut and no one in sight. I sit and wait, keeping the camera focused on the entrance. Once they open it, I'll be ready. But instead, I hear car doors slam and a truck drive away. They must have climbed up the hill while I was sneaking through the woods trying to stay hidden. Just then the dude with the muscles comes back into view. I start recording as he sits down and leans against the heavy wooden door. I wait. Nothing. He must be the watchman today. I stay a little longer to make sure nothing more will happen, then slowly make my way back to the trail and down the mountain to a safe spot.

My plan was to hike back up there several times over the next few days, snap pictures, and shoot some video. I had hoped with enough collected evidence the sheriff and my parents would have to believe me. But when I watch my video I realize the sound is worthless. I can't hear anything the guys are saying, just lots of squawking birds. The images of three men and a rifle could be a hunting party. Nothing incriminating.

Okay, I have until Saturday. But the boss man's remarks of an approaching storm bother me. If it rains or snows they'll see my footprints, and I know they'll have at least one guard walking around watching for intruders. And thanks to Sheriff Miller, they know I'm suspicious. But I've got to keep trying. I have to keep those drugs off the street before more innocent lives are ruined.

What I need is a backup plan. If a storm comes tonight, I can't go to the mine the way I did today. Not only would it be difficult to reach, but they'd spot my tracks. How else can I get there?

Suddenly, a whole new set of ideas formulates in my head. Inside. I could do it from the inside.

After a few minutes deciding on the details I walk toward town, nervous about what I have to do. I've never done any breaking and entering before. My rap sheet continues to grow.

As I near town I realize I've somehow become a part of this place. I want to help keep Silver Springs and its people safe. Who would've thought I'd come to care so much? I try to casually stroll down the wooden boardwalk, but am bothered by the judgmental looks thrown my way. A few weeks ago I wouldn't have cared what anyone here thought of me, but now I'm ashamed at what they must think. When I reach the library, I take a deep breath and enter. Lucky for me the place is busy.

I grab a book off a shelf and find an empty table near the office. Opening the book, I pretend to read. Sophie's mom comes out of her office.

When she sees me she stops, glances around, then walks over to me.

"I'm surprised to see you here, Jake."

"Hi, Mrs. Metcalf, how are you?"

"I'm okay, Jake. But what about you?"

"I've definitely had better weeks. Listen, for what it's worth, I don't do drugs. I honestly think whoever slashed my tires planted the weed," I say, feeling a need to explain myself to her.

She studies my face for a moment. "I hope you're telling the truth. I've always liked you, Jake."

"Thanks, I appreciate that."

"I'm usually a pretty good judge of character. Besides, I don't believe everything I read."

"I wish more people had that policy."

"If you've done nothing wrong, then you have nothing to feel bad about. Trust in God and the truth will come out in the end."

"I hope so."

Someone waves at her from the reference desk for assistance.

"Excuse me, Jake. Good luck."

"Thanks, Mrs. Metcalf," I answer as she walks away.

I pretend to read and hope Sophie doesn't come to volunteer today.

After awhile, a group of kids enter and ask Mrs. Metcalf for some help finding research materials. Perfect. That should keep her occupied. As she moves out of sight, I quickly get up and slip into her office.

I know the key to the tunnels is in here somewhere. I open drawers in search of it. I have no idea what I'll say if I get caught. Oh well . . . my reputation's trashed anyway. It's more important to help stop Deputy Grady and the others from spreading drugs around here. After a few minutes I come across a compartment with several keys in it. I grab the one labeled "tunnel" and also snatch an extra back door key, then stuff them in my pocket. Good thing she's organized. I slide back into my seat to finish my pretend reading.

When I leave the library, large white snowflakes swirl down from the sky. Well, the dudes were right. I'm glad I have another plan. Hope I can pull it off by Saturday. Saturday . . .

snow . . . that means if it snows enough the Snow Ball will also be on Saturday. That's two full days away. Maybe, if I'm not dead by then, I can still take Sophie. Keep dreaming. There's no way she'll trust me now. It'd take a miracle for her to forgive me. My shoulders slump as I walk home, more alone than ever.

At home my mom tries to have one of her one-on-one talks with me. She must have finally decided how to broach the subject of my falling-to-pieces life.

"How are you, Jake? We've been so focused on the fallout I haven't really checked on how you're holding up."

"I'm fine. Have you heard from Bill or Coach today?" Now that the whole sordid mess is in the paper, I'm sure there were even more phone calls today.

"The sponsors will be deciding soon. Their board members are meeting to discuss the situation. Bill says even a hint of a scandal makes companies nervous; he expects them to terminate the contracts for breaking the lifestyle clause. Coach has placed you on probation and is benching you from the European competition. He wants to meet with you next week."

Hopefully I'll be alive next week.

"Rachael and Tommy called. They both said they tried calling you."

"Yeah, too many calls and texts. I finally turned my cell off. Besides, there's no one I want to talk to right now."

"Your lawyer is working on an official statement. Any ideas for him?" Dad asks as he joins us.

"How about, I was set up?"

"He wants to keep focusing on that angle and the poor investigation by the sheriff's department, but after the hard time you had on the halfpipe last week he thinks people are likely to believe you are on something."

"*You* don't even think I'm telling the truth, why would anyone else?!"

"Jake, don't be angry. We believe you, but we're also worried. You have a lot going on. I wish you'd open up and talk to us," he says.

"Jake, we're very proud of you," Mom says. "We believe in you and will always stick by you. We moved here to regroup and get back to the kind of environment we used to have . . . community, church, friends. We all need the support that comes from those. And I've been thinking that it's time we all go back to church."

"Okay."

"If it's all too much—the training, sponsors, media—we'll figure it out together," Dad adds. "We don't care about any of the fame or money. We only care about you."

If they only knew the snowboarding load and my trashed reputation were the least of my problems at the moment. But they'd really think I'm smokin' something if I told them I'm about to risk my life to bring down drug smugglers who know I'm on to them.

"We're a family and we support each other—no matter what." Mom's eyes tear up.

"I know you guys do a ton for me, and I appreciate it all," I say as I hug Mom.

"Okay. Well, dinner will be ready soon. I made your favorite."

"Thanks." Like calzones will solve the problems of the world.

❄

Thursday morning and the newscasters break the news. Schools are cancelled. It has snowed all night and the blizzard will continue throughout the day. Looking out the window confirms it. There's nothing but white, and no way I can venture out in these conditions. Getting lost in zero visibility won't help the situation. I'll have to wait until it slows down a bit. Great.

I spend the day in my room going over the plan in my head. I pack my large hiking backpack with everything I think I could possibly need, and try to stay calm. The good news is, the illegal stash is probably unattended. No need to protect the stuff now. No one in their right mind would attempt to go up there today.

The storm doesn't let up the entire day. The snow just keeps piling up. Waiting out the weather is driving me crazy.

Finally around midnight the snow starts to slow, enough that I can see past the driveway. Somewhat confident that I won't totally lose my way, I sneak out into the cold night. With my fully loaded backpack in tow, I trudge through the heavy deep snow toward town. If I'm lucky I can get up to the mine, capture all the evidence I need without the guards lurking around, and return home before anyone knows I'm missing.

When I reach the library, thoroughly exhausted from struggling through thigh-high snowdrifts, I pull out the library key and unlock the door. The alarm starts to beep and I punch in the code Sophie once innocently shared with me. I stomp the snow off my boots and brush off my coat. Silently, I make my way across the library to the back wall where the hidden passageway is located. I push on the corner the way Sophie had done weeks before. Unbelievable how much has changed since then. The wall once again opens effortlessly. Then with a sign of the cross and a quick prayer for safety, I enter the hidden tunnel.

Trying to get my bearings, I stand completely still for a moment in the darkness. I don't want to turn on the light yet in case anyone happens to be out on the boardwalk in the middle of the night during a blizzard. Reality check . . . everyone else is safe and sound at home sleeping. I pull out my flashlight then close the door behind me. Using the small beam of light to guide me, I make my way across the room to the tunnel door. As I slip the key in the lock and turn the handle, a blast of musty air hits me. The consistent underground temperature makes it warmer in the tunnel than outside today.

I turn on the overhead light and check the tunnel map, which I studied all day, preparing for my mission. Sophie and I had explored the tunnel to the left, which leads out past the school. But today, I'm interested in the tunnel to the right which leads into the mine. According to the maps, this way will take me up through the mountain and then connect with the main tunnel of the mine. It appears that artery holds a track system on which carts were used to get the gold out of the mine. The tracks lead straight to the large entrance room at the top of the mine where the illegal operation is set up.

There are no lights hanging from the ceiling on this side of the tunnel. Not that I'm surprised. Sophie had told me it wasn't used anymore and was blocked due to safety issues. I have no idea what I'll find, but think I'm prepared. Besides my flashlight, I brought a battery-powered lantern that lights up a much greater area. The complete silence, except for my pounding heart, is eerie.

Turning on the lantern, I make my way down the cool tunnel, and it doesn't take long to reach a dead end. Old rotting boards are nailed in a crisscross pattern across the entryway. I place the lantern on the floor, then open up my backpack and pull out a crow bar. Good thing Mom didn't snoop today and open my bag. I would've had a lot to explain.

The boards are easy to pull off, but splinter in the process. I toss them off to the side. There's no door to deal with, only an old frame of heavy wooden beams that leads to complete darkness.

Peering into the pitch-black tunnel, I wonder if this is really such a great idea. But I push away the doubt and move forward slowly. The light from the lantern casts long shadows on the stone walls, illuminating the small circular holes that scatter the rock every few feet—evidence of the dynamite used long ago to make these tunnels.

Who knows what shape this place is in? No one has even been in this part of the mine in decades. As I move along, I create a map in my mind, taking inventory of every turn and obstacle, whether it's a rock or an old barrel. In case I need to make a quick escape, I want to be prepared.

Finally, I come to the end of this connecting tunnel. It opens up to the larger tunnel through which a narrow track runs down the center. I leave a glow stick here to mark the way back toward the library. The thought of missing the turn and instead following the track deeper into the mountain, where underground lakes or collapsed paths could lurk, almost makes me hyperventilate.

I focus on the old carts and mining tools that litter the side of the tunnel. Under different circumstances this place would be cool to explore. But not now. Again, I scan everything, memorizing every detail, each item and its location. Painstakingly I check the track, making mental notes of any broken areas. Usually I'm not such a detail freak, but if I'm running for my life, I don't want to trip on anything.

The whole tunnel gently slopes up toward the top of the mine, with the exception of one steep section. At the bottom of this sharp incline is a broken section of track; twisted metal shoots up in a menacing formation. At the top of this slope, the tunnel makes a left-hand turn and eventually starts to flatten out. Consulting the old map, I realize I'm getting close to the entryway. I turn off the lantern and stand quietly in complete darkness. After an eternity of nerve-racking silence, I'm convinced I'm alone, which should be comforting since I don't want to run into the bad guys, but instead gives me the creeps. I pull out my flashlight and continue on.

Eventually the claustrophobic tunnel opens up to a larger space. A search with the flashlight reveals towers of crates and large bulky duffle bags piled around the area. I made it. The tightness in my chest releases slightly. My idea actually worked!

They haven't moved out yet. One of the crates is open revealing bags of white powder, verifying my suspicions. I silently remove my backpack, push it in the shadows of the tunnel so I don't trip over it, then take a deep breath. Here's my chance. I've got a perfect shot. Sheriff Miller will have to believe me now. I turn the lantern back on, lighting the small entrance. With camera in hand I walk toward the open crate and snap photos of the white bags of powder that occupy it. I take pictures and video of the whole area, trying to capture the space as best as I can.

A check of my handiwork reveals I'm no cameraman. It's hard to see the whole scene in the photos. With a last-minute thought I pull out my phone, press the camera key, snap a photo of the area, and text it to Sophie, then shove it in my back pocket. I'm a bit surprised to get service inside the mountain. The picture isn't enough to make her suspect anything, just a little proof later when I try to explain myself and plead my case.

Checking the video, I see it's slightly better but only shows some wooden crates in a dark room. Hardly the proof I need to convince Sheriff Miller. Physical evidence would be better—I think I need to swipe a bag to show him and somehow convince him it's not mine. As I silently reach for one of the bags, a cold object jabs up against my neck. I freeze, and my heart leaps to my throat. I'm not alone.

"Where did you come from?" snarls the deputy as he pushes the barrel of his gun into my neck.

I'm such an idiot. Why did I assume they left the stash alone? Slowly, I raise my arms. How long has he been watching me?

"How'd you get here?" he asks again as he jams the metal further into my flesh. How'd I get here? Is it possible he didn't see me come out of the tunnels?

"Why are you doing this? Aren't you supposed to uphold the law?" I ask, ignoring his question.

"Yeah, but this pays a whole lot better."

He slams the handle of the gun into my jaw. My head snaps back and I taste blood. I draw back and throw a punch at his weaselly face. My fist smacks into his right eye. His head flies back from the force and causes him to stumble backward. I turn to lunge for the tunnel when I hear the sickening sound of a gun cocking.

"Move and you die."

I freeze.

"Lose the cameras."

I slowly bend down and place them on the ground, then turn to face him. He's squinting and tearing up, the skin around his eye is red from the impact. Blood begins to drip down his cheek from a nasty looking cut. My throbbing fist suddenly hurts less after seeing the damage it has done.

"You've been nothing but a pain in my life since you moved to town. Here, make yourself useful," he says as he tosses me a roll of duct tape. Then at gunpoint he makes me tear off a long strip of tape for him to secure my hands behind my back.

"You know, you only have yourself to blame. I tried to keep you away from all this. But you wouldn't listen."

After he tapes up my hands, he shoves me against the rock wall. As I slide down to sit against the cold stone floor, the partially opened mine door is silhouetted as the blackness of the night transforms to dull grays. Friday morning has arrived.

He binds my feet together, then, cursing up a storm, roots through a backpack on the other side of the space while dabbing at his cheek. Must be his backpack since mine is still hidden. I realize with a glimmer of hope my cell phone is in my back pocket. Is it possible to make a call? If I squirm enough I think I can reach it.

With limited mobility I'm not sure I can access my call list to reach my parents or the keypad to place a 911 call. But my phone should still be open to my text screen from the message I just sent Sophie. Texting her is the only option. I'm pretty sure there's no way to find the right keys to type a message. But what else can I do?

I didn't want her involved, but maybe she'll call the sheriff. Will she even look at a message from me? I'll have to try. I don't have any other options.

But what if the deputy hears me? He'll read the message and know I sent out a call for help. Sophie would be in danger. That leaves one option—the '49ers' code.

Chapter 16

Sophie

"Sophie, Sophie! It's another snow day!! Come on! Get up!" Sam abruptly wakes me on Friday morning as he jumps on my bed. He's quickly followed by a snow-covered Everest. She loves the snow almost as much as my brother.

I push the wet dog off my bed and mumble an unenthusiastic, "Yippee."

He doesn't wait for any more response and zips out of my room, Everest hot on his heels.

The stupid snow started Wednesday afternoon and continued to fall through the night and all day yesterday, causing the schools to be shut down. In fact, a total blizzard hit the area. What did I ever do to deserve this?

My phone buzzed the entire day on Thursday with everyone texting and bubbling with excitement about the dumb dance. I got sick of hearing about it and finally turned my phone off. It's the first time ever I'm not eager for the Snow Ball. Thanks a lot, Jake. The only good thing about the blizzard is that no one was talking about me ruining Jake's life.

Every time I looked out the window yesterday it was like someone picked up a giant snow globe and shook it hard. In fact, when I went to bed it was still snowing. Geez, enough already, I get it. The Snow Ball is going to happen whether I want it to or not.

I get dressed then head downstairs. Dad and Sam are eating breakfast.

"Hey, kiddo. It finally stopped snowing, but schools are closed again due to the high snowdrifts and because of some electrical problems at the high school," Dad informs me.

"Everyone will be disappointed if they have to postpone the dance," Mom adds.

"Yeah, real disappointing." Maybe this is the lucky break I need.

"Are you excited for the dance?" Mom asks.

"Not really," I reply, avoiding her eyes.

"Is that because of Jake?" she asks.

"You're not still interested in him, are you? Don't you see the mess he's in?" Dad joins the conversation.

Could this be any more humiliating?

"Don't worry, Dad. I'm not interested in Jake." I want to say more about what a jerk he is, but my prayer request to keep from judging others pops into my mind. Remember, Sophie, let those without sin cast the first stone. So I keep quiet.

"Honey, what happened? I thought you two liked each other," Mom says.

"She has better judgment than to hang out with some-one who does drugs. Now I don't have to forbid her from seeing him," Dad says.

"Sophie," Mom says, ignoring my dad, "are you sure? I saw him at the library on Wednesday and he proclaimed his innocence. He seemed really genuine. Maybe he *was* set up."

Unbelievable; she's still on his side?

"Jake told me he doesn't want to see me anymore so it doesn't matter."

"Hmm, strange. I thought he liked you."

"Yeah, me too."

I hate to admit it because I despise him for using me to boost his ego, but I still think he's actually innocent of the whole drug thing. Remembering how sincere he seemed when we talked about using his talents for good and his story about Rachael and her friend Emma, I don't believe he'd get messed up with that junk.

I spend the morning building snowmen and forts in the backyard with Sam. Then around lunchtime, after peeling off a wet layer of clothes, we drag into the kitchen. Mom is busy cooking, and from the large quantities of appetizers that line the counters I'd say the Snow Ball preparations are proceeding on schedule.

"Good news. They got the problem fixed at the school so the Snow Ball is on for tomorrow," explains my mom.

Fantastic.

When the phone rings my mom pleads for me to answer it since she's in the middle of rolling out dough.

"Hello?"

"Sophie? It's Mrs. Taylor; I'm so glad you're home. I really need to speak with you." She sounds a little panicky.

Taking my sandwich and the kitchen phone, I go up to my room. Whatever this is about, I don't need eavesdroppers.

"How can I help you, Mrs. Taylor?"

"Jake's missing."

"What?"

"We haven't seen him since last night. He disappeared sometime after ten o'clock. We've tried calling him, but he doesn't answer his phone. We're worried sick. What if he's lost in the snow somewhere?" Her voice trembles.

Wow. That's weird, but I don't quite get where I fit in.

"Did you tell the sheriff?"

"Yes, and he said he'll do what he can, which isn't much since Jake hasn't been gone very long. He's going to request a signal trace on Jake's cell phone, but because of the blizzard the process may take awhile. I'm just so worried. Jake wouldn't leave without telling us. And if he wanted to get away he would've taken his jeep."

"Well, I haven't seen him since Sunday."

"But you were the last person he sent a text to, early this morning. We checked his account online. I was hoping maybe he said something to you that would help us figure out where he is."

Why would he text me?

"Hang on a sec and I'll look." I grab my phone from my desk, turn it on, and check. Sure enough, two texts from Jake. I stare at them. Weird.

"Well, he sent me two messages. One is some kind of dark photo that I can't make out. And the other is useless. It just says 'double black diamond.' I don't know what that means."

"Oh." Her sadness makes me feel horrible.

"If I hear from him, I'll tell him to call you."

"Thanks, Sophie. You know, nobody around here really knows him. He's a very sweet kid. The past year has been incredibly hard on all of us. He didn't know how to handle all the attention thrown at him. That's why we moved here, so we could all get back to a wholesome environment and focus on the values and morals we believe are important." She starts to cry.

Not sure why she's telling me all this, but I guess she needs to vent.

"The sheriff thinks he ran off because he's facing so much trouble. But I don't believe he ran away," Mrs. Taylor continues. "His boots, winter coat, and hiking backpack are gone, but he didn't take anything else. Something's wrong."

"I wish I could help you."

"I was hoping you might know something. I know he likes you a lot."

He sure has a funny way of showing it.

I tell her I'll keep her posted if I hear anything, then we hang up. Jake, you selfish jerk! How can you worry your sweet mother like this?

The phone, still clutched in my hand, rings again. I quickly answer, hoping it might be Jake.

"Hello?"

"Um, hi," says a deep male voice. "Is this Sophie?"

"Yes."

"This is Gary, your dad's colleague down in Denver."

"Oh, hi." It takes me a moment to remember who Gary is. "Thanks for running all that lab work for me. That was really nice." Not to mention a waste of his time.

"Anytime, it's always a nice distraction to work on something besides my research. I wanted to let you know we got the autopsy results back from the rabbit."

"Let me guess—Thumper died of old age."

"Not exactly. He actually died from a cocaine overdose."

My mouth falls open.

"What? The bunny was a junkie?"

"Apparently," he laughs. "It's pretty strange, though. I wonder where a rabbit could have come across cocaine."

"I think I might know," I say, thinking of those crazy hikers who were so high they claimed a ghost chased them out of the mine. "Well, thanks for letting me know."

"Sure, hope it helps," he says as he hangs up.

Not likely. I doubt forest animals accidentally getting high is the next Watergate. Poor unlucky bunny. But the bigger mystery is: what happened to Jake?

It doesn't make sense for him to worry his mom and dad. He told me he appreciates all they do for him. If so, why would he take off with no explanation?

I re-check his text: double black diamond. What does that mean? Why would he even bother to write that and send it to me? The term double black diamond means the hardest

226

ski and snowboard runs. Was he trying to tell me he went snowboarding? In a blizzard? In the middle of the night? Yeah, right.

When I take a closer look at the photo he sent, I realize it's not completely black. More like shades of grey. I stare at it but can't see anything on my tiny phone screen. I transfer it to my computer and use my photo software to lighten it. Adjusting the settings causes some shapes to form, but I still can't tell what I'm looking at. It appears to be some boxes piled on top on each other and a dark wall. What the heck?

Trying to sort things out, I lie on my bed and stare at the ceiling. Jake's missing. He sent me a message that makes no sense and a dark, nondescript photo. Why would he send them to *me*? He kicked me to the curb in no uncertain terms, although I'm still not sure why. I thought things had been going well. What happened?

I replay the last few times I saw him in my head. Saturday had been awesome. He really acted like he liked me. Then he was pulled over by the deputy and got his ticket. Sunday when I called him he was down, but still sounded okay. In fact he thanked me for believing in him. And why bother agreeing to meet me at the mill if he no longer liked me? He could have given me his good-bye speech on the phone. Did something happen after we hung up to change his mind? Maybe his coach thought his focus should be on his training and not on me. Could that stupid magazine article have something to do with his change in attitude? He dumped me before it came out, but maybe he knew about it before it was published.

The trashy tabloid still lies crinkled in the corner where I threw it. I grab it, still surprised I'm in the thing. This time as I study the picture something in the background catches my eye. I hadn't noticed it before because I was too shocked to see my face on the glossy pages. In the photo, the sunlight shines off of something behind my shoulder. The door of the mine is behind me. What would be catching the light? I check my photos from the day I collected samples at the mine and see a silver chain and lock. That definitely wasn't there when I took the photos of the mine last spring. At that time there was an old rusty chain; I remember because I liked how authentic it looked. This new shiny silver thing totally messes up the picture. I must have been too distracted the last few times I was there to notice it. How long has it been there? Deputy Grady said he was patrolling the area. Maybe he replaced it.

I grab the phone and call over to the sheriff's office.

"Hello, Sheriff's Station. Sheriff Miller here."

"Oh, hi, Sheriff Miller. This is Sophie Metcalf."

"Sophie! How are you?"

"Good. Hey, um, I talked to Mrs. Taylor this afternoon and she's really worried about Jake. I thought I'd see if you heard anything new."

"I feel bad for her, but I think Jake's just out of control. There's nothing to indicate foul play. He's under a lot of pressure; maybe he's off somewhere getting high."

"Jake doesn't do drugs."

"I know you like him, but drugs would explain his behavior lately. He definitely hasn't been acting like himself.

In fact, he called me the other day with a crazy story about Deputy Grady. I think he was trying to blame someone else to save himself from the mess he's in."

"What did he say about Deputy Grady?"

"I'm sorry, Sophie, but I won't repeat ridiculous theories that could smear his good name."

"Oh. Okay. There's something else I wanted to ask you. Did you change the locks at the mine?"

"No. That would fall under the Park Service duties. Why?"

"I noticed in some pictures I took that there's a new shiny chain and lock on the mine entrance. When Jake and I ran into Deputy Grady that day, he said something about vandalism. I was thinking maybe whoever was messing with the mine was the same one who took a knife to Jake's tires."

"Vandalism? I haven't heard about any vandalism at the mine. Of course, Deputy Grady has been working with the Park Service. He has a buddy there. Maybe he forgot to log it in. I'll have to ask him about it when he gets back."

"Back from where?"

"He was called away for a few days to tend to a sick relative. That's just like him, always helping people out. Well, Sophie, I should go. You wouldn't believe how busy things get when it snows."

"Thanks, Sheriff Miller."

I wish I could remember what the deputy had said about vandalism. Seems strange the sheriff wouldn't know anything about it. And I can't believe Jake called the sheriff accusing Deputy Grady of something. At the diner, Jake said he thought the deputy was out to get him. Talk about paranoid.

Jake's words—about there being two sides to every story and a good reporter would investigate both—bounce around my head. Maybe there's more going on here than meets the eye. I misjudged Jake once and don't want to make that mistake again.

Why did Jake think the deputy was up to something? The last time I saw Deputy Grady was when he caught me messing with the life-size Jake display on Tuesday at the drug-store. Totally embarrassing. He was nice though and I didn't get in trouble.

Why didn't Jake like him? Everyone likes the deputy. Everyone . . . except Everest. I flash back on Everest growling and snarling at him. She's never done anything like that before. Could she have sensed something? His explanation that he had caught a raccoon for Mrs. Meyer made sense at the time.

I grab the phone to make another call.

"Hello?"

"Mrs. Meyer? Hi, it's Sophie."

"Oh, hi, dear. How are you?"

"I'm good. Thanks. How are you?"

"Well, my arthritis always acts up a bit when it snows, but otherwise I'm well. Is there something I can help you with?"

"I know this is a strange question, but did Deputy Grady help you recently trap raccoons?"

"No. I haven't had any troubles with them since the spring. My son helped me pick out a new critter-proof trash can."

"Oh. I thought I heard you were still having raccoon problems."

"None at all. If the coons are bothering you, I can tell you where to get one of these wonderful trash cans. They come in different colors."

"Thanks, I'll keep that in mind. By the way, how's Duchess?"

"Oh, much better, dear; her strange symptoms are gone. Thanks for asking."

"Sure, sorry to bother you. Bye."

Okay, that's weird. Why would Deputy Grady have lied about trapping raccoons? He was being really nice that day, giving me maps to other 4x4 trails for Jake and me to explore. I glance at the magazine spread open on my bed. Or . . . he gave me the maps to keep us away from the mine. Interesting coincidence—the deputy is out of town when Jake is missing.

I grab my phone and stare once again at the photo and text Jake sent me. He only sent them to me. If he really wanted to get away from here, why would he send them to me? *What am I missing, Jesus? God, please help me figure this out.*

Double Black Diamond. An expert ski run. What else could it mean? The light bulb in my brain suddenly turns on. *Thank you, Jesus!* Maybe he was using a code. The '49ers' would have double meanings for the words they chose. Diamond. Gems? Girl's best friend? Sparkling jewel? Shimmering rock?

Shimmering rock. I told him that's how Silver Springs got its name, from the shimmering rocks in the stream, and that I thought it looked like diamonds. Is he talking about Silver Springs? Where in Silver Springs?

Drawn to my desk, I stare at the enhanced photo again. Where was this taken? Crates piled up against a dark wall. I continue to brighten and zoom, but it only makes the background blurry. The wall doesn't look smooth. It looks rough, almost like the sides of the tunnel behind the library.

Oh gosh. This photo is in the tunnel somewhere. Of course. Diamonds come from mines. Suddenly things come together in my mind—the deputy's lie, the crazy story of the hikers chased out of the mine, the new heavy chain, Jake's suspicions. These crates must be up in the mine entrance.

Could Deputy Grady be involved in something illegal? Did Jake figure it out? Why didn't he tell anyone?

He did. Jake told Sheriff Miller, who didn't believe him.

Am I losing my mind? None of this makes sense. But what if Jake is in trouble? If Deputy Grady is involved, then Jake must have felt he couldn't tell anyone till he had proof. And proof of what? What could be in those crates? Weapons? Money? Drugs? Drugs. Cocaine. The dead bunny. Suddenly Big Jim's words come back to me. A drug problem. No one knows the source.

Double Black Diamond. Are there any other meanings? I google "double black diamond." It means "extreme difficulty."

Jake, what are you trying to tell me? Are you in the mine? Do you need help? I throw up a quick prayer, *O Lord, please keep Jake safe.* Even though he doesn't really like me, I don't want anything bad to happen to him. What can I do? The sheriff won't believe me any more than he did Jake. Deputy Grady is his protégé. Besides, how can I convince anyone else of this situation when I'm not sure I believe it? Can I get to the top of the mine to check it out? No way with all this snow. How did Jake get there? His mom mentioned he left sometime Thursday night. Most of the snow had already fallen by then, so it would have been nearly impossible to hike up there. And besides, he would have left tracks. If he was trying to get proof of something illegal, he would have been hiding and wouldn't risk making a trail through the snow. Where could he have hidden?

The tunnels. He knows they lead to the mine entrance. And Mom said he had been at the library. Would he have tried to use them to get up there?

By the time I figure things out, it's dark. I try texting Jake several times but never hear back from him. During dinner I contemplate telling my parents, but decide it sounds too crazy. And what would they do even if they did believe me? Contact the sheriff, and he'll think both Jake and I have lost touch with reality. Everyone else in town thinks the deputy is extremely helpful and Jake is a messed-up stoner. They won't believe it without proof. So I keep my mouth shut.

Finally, when the house is quiet after everyone goes to bed, I lie awake trying to figure things out. Could it really be possible, or is my wild imagination out of control? However, if Jake is in trouble the right thing to do—what I *want* to do—is help. Me against some crooks. I feel sick to my stomach, realizing I'm the only one who can do anything. A panic washes over me. I'm not brave enough. But I've got to think of something. He's counting on me.

Okay, God, help me out here. If you can use me to help Jake, please give me wisdom and strength.

I keep repeating my prayer until, in the wee hours of the morning, a rescue plan forms in my mind.

Quiet as a mouse, I sneak around the house to raid Sam's scout survival pack and root through the garage for items I may need. I leave a note on the kitchen counter stating I woke early, went on a walk, and may stop at Kate's on the way home. Hopefully that will curb their curiosity for awhile. As the first sunlight of Saturday morning lightens the sky, I pull on my boots and walk down the deserted streets to the library. I don't have the key to the library so when I get there I take an old brick from my bag and throw it through the glass window of the back door. Sorry, Mom, someone's life may be at stake.

Careful not to cut myself, I reach in and unlock the door. I notice the alarm doesn't go off. I hurry into Mom's office to grab the key to the tunnel. It's not here. Maybe I'm not crazy after all. Intrigued, I check out the secret panel, quickly enter, and close it behind me. The tunnel door stands open. No key needed today. That discovery and the lights that greet me help to confirm my thoughts. Someone has been here. Then I do something I've only done one other time—head to the right, toward the mine.

With no lights to brighten the area, I've always found this unlit part of the tunnel creepy. Something about the boarded-up mine is frightening. Who knows what dangers lurk behind the barricade? With my flashlight clasped in my hand, I try to push my fears away and bravely walk toward the mine, ignoring the strange shadows.

Come on, Sophie. You can accomplish anything through Christ who gives you strength.

When I come to the heavy beam doorway I know I'm right. The boards that usually block the way have been pried off and thrown into a pile. Jake has gone up the tunnel. I slowly pass through the entrance, remembering the definition of Double Black Diamond—extreme difficulty. Even with my dad's brightest flashlight this place is terrifying. I almost turn back from this insane mission when another possibility comes to mind. Jake could be hurt. Maybe he fell down a shaft or is trapped in a rock collapse. Anything could have happened. Pushing my fears aside, I concentrate on Jake and move forward into the darkness.

Chapter 17

Jake

How am I ever going to get out of this? I've been stuck in this miserable mine sitting on this cold rock floor all day. I'm guessing it's now Friday night around midnight, which means it has been twenty-four hours since I snuck out of my house—officially making this the longest and worst day of my life. All I can do is sit and think back on this day.

After Deputy Dirtbag found me, he messed with his injury then started screaming into his phone. This gave me the time to try contacting Sophie. Getting the phone out of my back pocket, turning the screen on, and texting all with my wrists taped together behind my back was quite a challenge. I'm surprised my shoulder didn't pop out of joint as I strained to see the screen. Thankfully my phone has a sliding keyboard I was able to access.

After I texted Sophie, I sat there contemplating how to get the deputy to release my hands so I could fight my way out of this before his cronies show up. He must have drawn the short end of the stick and got the job of watching the illegal stash during the blizzard till the others could get back with the truck. If his buddies were sticking with their original plan, they'd be back sometime on Saturday. While Silver Springs danced the night away; these guys would be moving all the crates and closing up shop here. No one ever the wiser.

Before I could come up with a plan, the mine door opened and this guy in a huge parka stomped through the door. My hopes of turning the situation around disappeared. Now I was outnumbered, making any escape infinitely harder. The guy shook the snow off his coat and pulled back his hood. Realizing it was the tat-covered guy made me feel somewhat better. He seemed less evil than Muscles or Boss man.

"I did what you asked and double-checked—there's no one else around. I think he's alone," he said as he blinked, his eyes trying to adjust to the darkness of the mine. "Geez, what happened to your eye?"

"Shut up, Tony."

"Why didn't you use your handcuffs on him?" Tony asked as he scrutinized me.

"Gee, why didn't I think of that? Why would I need them here, you idiot? They're at home with my uniform."

"So how'd he get here?"

"I don't know. I was napping behind the crates when suddenly I look up and there he is. But it's time to find out," he said as they both approached me.

I realized he had no idea how I got here. Maybe Sheriff Miller never told him about the tunnels. At least I had one advantage. They wouldn't be expecting me to use the tunnels to escape if I managed to get loose.

"So don't make us beat it out of you; how'd you get in here?" They hovered over me; trying to intimidate me. It worked.

"I snuck in the door." I tried to play it cool and not let them see how scared I was. I didn't want to give them any more of an upper hand than they already had.

"We shouldn't have left the door open all night," said Tony.

"We had to, otherwise the huge drifts would have blocked the door and trapped us in here, moron."

"I've been searching the area for hours. I didn't see any footprints except my own."

"The snow's my comfort zone. I snowshoed in from the road, then boarded down and buried my stuff so you wouldn't see it," I said, hoping they wouldn't want to know where I "hid" my stuff.

"You obviously didn't do a very good job of checking the area. I'm always havin' to clean up your messes," the deputy snarled. "First you guys leave the mine unattended and those hikers come wandering in, then you lose that bag of coke, now this. I'm sick of covering for you."

"Hey, I came up with the plan of scaring those guys. You have to admit it worked. And I keep telling you we didn't lose that bag. We knew it fell out of the crate. But it's not my fault a squirrel ran off with it. What was I supposed to do—search the whole forest for it?!" Tony argued back.

"It wasn't very difficult to track down, since the stupid rodent dragged the bag along the ground tearing a hole in it. There was a nice, white, powdery trail from here to the stream.

Then I had to clean up all the animals that died from eating the junk."

"How is that my fault? Besides, it was your idea to get rid of the rest of it by pouring it in the stream."

"What else was I supposed to do? The coke was no longer pure," Deputy Grady hissed.

"So what're we going to do with him?"

Deputy Grady ignored him and instead turned back to interrogating me. "How'd you figure it out, Hotshot?"

"Maybe you shouldn't have been boasting so much about how you slashed my tires," I answered.

"Maybe you need to learn a lesson about eavesdropping on other people's conversations. Did you tell anyone else?"

I wasn't sure whether to let him think someone may come looking for me or tell him I acted alone. If they thought I was a lone wolf then maybe they'd let their guard down and I could make a move. On the other hand, if they thought people would be searching for me then they couldn't as easily kill me and get away with it.

"I left a note to come looking for me up here if I disappear. I tried to tell Sheriff Miller, but it seems everyone thinks you're Silver Spring's number-one citizen and I'm a junkie," I answered.

"It's easy to fool people. Just be helpful and they'll trust you forever," he smirked.

"Should we call Bowers?" Tony asked. "He said we'd have to take care of the kid if he caused any more problems."

I eyed the tunnel and wondered what my chances were of making it down with my feet bound together and my hands duct taped behind my back. Probably not great, but that had to be better than staying here, waiting for them to off me.

Then the deputy gave me a glimmer of hope. "Maybe there's another possibility."

I perked up at that.

"What?" asked Tony.

"He's worth a boatload of money. What if we hold him hostage and get some ransom money for him? This could be our secret. We wouldn't have to tell the others."

They both stared at me.

"Do you think it would work?" asked Tony.

"Sure. I bet his mommy and daddy would be willing to do almost anything for their precious boy. If we got enough dough for him, maybe we could even get out of dealing drugs."

"How much could we get for him?" Tony looked me up and down like a farmer at auction checking over the cattle.

"At least several hundred thousand. A million? I don't know exactly."

"Where could we hide him?"

"We could gag him and push him back into those dark tunnels. No one would be the wiser. After we move the goods, we can come back for him."

"I don't know. Maybe we should just tell Bowers."

"We could make a lot of easy money, Tony."

While they were debating what to do with me, the bright morning sunlight began to stream in through the partially-opened mine door. Suddenly my phone began to vibrate. Most likely my parents. Unfortunately, against the rock floor the vibration echoed through the enclosed space.

Their heads snapped in my direction, then they looked at each other.

"Didn't you search him?" Tony asked.

"I was a little busy tying him up by myself."

Tony yanked me up by the arm, then grabbed my phone. Deputy Grady frisked me, then shoved me back down.

"Oh, it's his mommy calling. How sweet."

Mom must be frantic. Whose bright idea was it to sneak off without leaving a note behind anyway?

"Check and see if he called anyone," ordered the deputy.

"Some message to a Sophie. Doesn't make any sense. The phone's about dead anyway."

Deputy Grady grabbed my cell and shoved it in his pocket. Good thing I used a code for my secret SOS.

"Jake, you don't need to worry about Sophie missing you. Don't know what you did to her, but boy was she mad. You know what they say about a woman scorned," Grady informed me.

I sent a quick thank-you prayer to God for keeping her safe.

"You should really treat girls with a little more respect," Tony added.

Great. Relationship advice from one of America's most wanted.

"You're lucky it was just your sunglasses display she went after," Grady said.

I couldn't help but grin, wondering what she did.

"Yeah, the next time it could be your jeep she attacks."

"That's what you two are for," I snapped, trying to sound tough and not scared out of my freakin' mind.

They both stared at me, then burst out laughing.

For the rest of the day, I kept trying to find a way to surreptitiously get my feet and hands free so I could escape, but they were always watching. Not sure it was the right decision to let them think someone may be coming because they never let their guard down. They gave me food, water, and even a blanket, but they never took their eyes, or weapons, off of me. The only time both my hands and feet were free was when they led me outside to take a leak. And then they both had their guns drawn.

As the hours wore on and the late afternoon light faded, I came to the conclusion no help was coming. Sophie must not have figured it out. Maybe she got the message, but it was too vague and she couldn't decipher it. Or maybe she was so mad at me she didn't bother to even read it. Whatever the case, I realized I wouldn't be rescued. If Sophie had figured out the message, she would've sent help by now. I shouldn't have tried to do this on my own. What was I thinking?

❄

I come back to the present and notice how darkness blankets the area. My options, as I see them, are not great. Either I make a break for it outside when my hands and feet are free—but face two guys with guns and three feet of snow—or I can attempt to go down the pitch-black tunnel with arms and legs bound. Neither seems likely to succeed. But I've got to try something, because if these two don't decide to go with the kidnapping scheme, when Bowers and the other crooks find me here tomorrow, I'm dead.

How did I go from having it all to this? Where did I go wrong? Life was good before the Olympics. Jon and Rick had been decent friends then. I always thought they were jealous and were the ones who changed when I got back. But maybe I was being a jerk like Sophie said, driving around town in my tricked-out jeep like I owned the place. As much as I'd like to blame the whole friendship debacle on them, I probably wasn't much of a friend to them.

Truth is, I've coasted since the Olympics. When the pressure hit last week, I couldn't handle it and freaked. Is that really who I've become? What happened to the kid who did things for others simply because it was the right thing to do? What happened to the person who worked hard in school, in sports, in life? If I get out of this situation in one piece I'll gladly take it, stress and all. I'm not gonna back down from the challenge.

And no more whining about living in Silver Springs. Ironically, I complained because this town was boring. I wouldn't mind a little boring about now. When I longed for excitement, running into drug traffickers wasn't what I had in mind.

Most importantly, if I hadn't moved here I never would have met Sophie. First thing I'm going to do if I get out of here is explain everything to her and tell her how I really feel. Her words about God's specialty being his ability to clean up our messes come to mind. I close my eyes and completely humble myself in prayer.

Okay, God, I could really use some help here. I've pretty much hit rock bottom and everything I try seems to fail. In fact I've made it all worse. I know I've screwed up, ignored you, treated friends badly, taken my talents for granted, and become an egotistical jerk. Is that what you want me to learn, to not just think of myself? To appreciate what you've done for me? Okay, I got the message. I really have. I see that everything is a gift that can be gone in an instant. And that the most important things in my life are my parents, friends, and you. Thank you for guiding me, protecting me, and helping me to see the truth. Now . . . how about a little help getting out of this mess? Amen.

I try to force myself to stay awake, but the lack of sleep and adrenaline-drain finally get to me. Maybe I should rest. I'll need my energy tomorrow when I make my big escape. Sick of leaning against the cold wall and hard crates, I slump to the floor. As I fall asleep I think about Sophie's wavy brown hair, those beautiful green eyes of hers, and her endless rambling stories.

Chapter 18

Sophie

My heart pounds so loudly in my chest as I make my way up the tunnel that I swear I hear it echoing off the rock walls. I wish I could move faster, but I'm terrified of what I may come across. As a result, the going is slow. I'm most afraid I'll stumble into a huge hole and fall hundreds of feet down into the mine. Plunging to my death does not sound like a good way to go. Although when you think about it, is there really any good way to die?

Other things worry me as well—like hordes of rats, falling rocks, or finding Jake hurt somewhere along the way. Maybe I should turn back and get help, but I'm not sure anyone will believe me. I mean seriously, it is kind of a tall tale. And besides, if Jake did discover some crime the deputy was involved in, then time could be of the essence. I force myself to continue climbing the cold dark tunnel.

A strange, eerie green glow begins to fill the tunnel as I move along. What is that? Some kind of chemical? With a death grip on the flashlight I stealthily advance. My path dead-ends at another tunnel where the green tint originates from. A huge gush of air escapes my lungs as I realize a fading green glow stick is the culprit. I didn't even know I had been holding my breath. This must be Jake's version of breadcrumbs to mark his way.

Shaking the cramp out of my right hand, I transfer my trusty flashlight to my left hand to scan the area. A railroad track runs down the center of this tunnel. I turn toward the left and head up the mountain. Don't even want to think what could be to the right, too many unknowns.

Rusty old mining cars and equipment litter the way. A broken section of track creates a horrifying shadow on the stone wall. No sign of an injured Jake though. I can't help but wonder when the last time someone was in here—besides me and probably Jake. It's got to be nearly one hundred years since any miners worked the area. Creepy.

Being inside this mountain is beyond terrifying, but I'm comforted by my prayers and the tracking beacon I grabbed from Sam's scout stuff. And, in trying to think of every possibility, I left my parents a second note in my room, where they won't look for it right away. In the event something happens to me they can find my location—hopefully.

As the climb continues I'm thrilled yet nervous to see light ahead. All this darkness is getting to me, but I'm scared about what I'll find. My heart almost leaps out of my chest when I reach the end of this artery and see the mine entrance. I actually made it to the top. Huge crates are piled around the area. Then I spot Jake. I found him! I can't believe it—he's actually here! Lying on the ground. Not moving. Oh no, is he hurt? Is he breathing? Am I too late? At last his shoulder moves slightly. I close my eyes in relief. He's asleep.

But a closer look shows his hands tied behind his back, causing a chill to run down my spine. His ankles also have been bound together. He's definitely in trouble.

That's when I hear the low voices. Two men stand by the open mine door. In my excitement to see Jake I hadn't noticed them. I stare at the guns in their hands. One is Deputy Grady—the creep. Jake was right about him. That slimy deputy had everyone fooled, especially Sheriff Miller. The usually tidy deputy looks horrible, his right eye discolored and swollen and his cheek smeared with blood. I sure hope that was courtesy of Jake.

No time to turn back and get help; they might do something horrible to him before I return. I've got to help Jake. What should I do first? Distract those two or free Jake? I figure I better start with Jake; he'll need to be able to move. As hard as I concentrate, willing him to wake up doesn't work. So much for telepathy. Crouching down, I feel around on the ground and grab some tiny pebbles. I zing them at Jake's face. He stirs.

"Jake," I whisper, glancing at the door to make sure the two creeps don't hear me.

Nothing. I try another pebble.

"Jake." How can he sleep at a time like this?

When the third pebble hits him he slowly opens his eyes and struggles to sit up. He grimaces as he rolls his shoulder. Dried blood snakes down from the corner of his mouth. He's hurt. What did they do to him? I toss another one. It hits him on the cheek. He glances my way. Finally! Then he looks back at the two men with guns. He mustn't be able to see me in the shadows. I try again.

"Jake."

This time he squints into the tunnel. I move forward, hoping he'll be able to see me while still staying out of view from the other two. His eyes widen as it registers I'm here. He gives me a quick smile then scoots his body closer to the tunnel, his back to me. His wrists are wrapped in duct tape. I root around in my backpack and grab Sam's pocketknife. With trembling hands I attempt to cut through the tape without cutting Jake. Free at last, he rubs his wrists but keeps them behind his back for appearance's sake.

Jake looks at me probably ready to make an escape, but his ankles are still taped together. I don't see any way to work on them without the guys with very large weapons noticing. Time for a distraction. I put my hand up, indicating for him to wait.

As I grab my backpack and sink into the shadows of the tunnel the men approach Jake.

"Morning, Sleeping Beauty," says the man I don't recognize. "Well, I guess you're wondering what we decided. We can't double-cross Bowers. He's not someone you want to mess with, if ya know what I mean. But maybe he'll be interested in the whole kidnapping scheme."

Not waiting to hear who this Bowers is, I silently move on. I have a plan, but it all depends on something I'm not even sure exists. When brainstorming about how I could save Jake, I immediately wondered what Sally would do. Hoping the legend is correct, I follow along the rock wall past the tunnel in search of the secret lookout area that Sally and her dad had made. They used it a century ago to watch for bandits, but today it may help us escape.

When I was little I thought the mine looked like a guardian angel overlooking the town. Well, I hope our guardian angels and the mine protect us now. I round a bend and, sure enough, small streams of light penetrate the darkness. The small slit in the rock is overgrown and snow blocks the narrow opening. I slide my fingers through the crack to clear some space. Peering out I see the mine entrance to the right.

Okay. Here goes. First, I pull out my cell and make a call. *Please, God, help this work.* Then taking a deep breath, I reach into my bag and grab the old firecrackers I found in the garage. I'd say this counts as an emergency. I squeeze my hand through the open space, then one at a time light them with my dad's fire pit lighter. As the flame burns down the fuse I fling them as far as I can, hoping they don't burn out in the snow. But it works perfectly. They start to pop before hitting the ground. That should get the attention of Deputy Grady and his partner.

I run back to Jake hoping he's using the distraction to free his ankles. But I freak at what I see. His partner must have run outside like I predicted, but Deputy Grady has his gun drawn and is heading toward Jake. No! You were supposed to run outside, you idiot! I look around and grab whatever I can find. Somehow I've got to help.

I watch in amazement as Jake swings his taped legs around, knocking the deputy's feet out from under him. The gun goes off as he falls with a thud. The deafening crack stuns me. I watch in amazement as Jake kicks the gun out of his hands. Deputy Grady doesn't give up though and lunges at Jake. I jump out of the shadows and swing the old, rusty shovel I grabbed as hard as I can. BAM! I hit him right in the stomach, so hard my hands vibrate. Stunned, he reels backward clutching his stomach, but he doesn't fall. Jake gets to his knees and throws a punch, right to the face. The dual blows knock him out.

We did it! Jake sits back down and smiles at me. I grab the pocket knife and work on freeing his ankles while he reaches into Deputy Grady's pocket and grabs his cell phone.

"Nice move," he says, then adds, "who's outside? I hope you brought the cavalry."

Uh oh. He expected me to bring help. "No one. I pulled a Sally," I say apologetically.

He grins and shakes his head.

"Let's get out of here," he says as he grabs my hand.

"We need them to follow us down the tunnel," I answer.

"Hurry and head down. Don't worry. I'll be right behind," he says as he pushes me back into the tunnel.

With a nod I turn around trusting he has a plan. I hurry down the tunnel, careful not to slide while staying against the wall. The eerie green glow is now my beacon of hope. At the glow stick I head toward the library. When I reach the large wooden doorway where Jake ripped off the keep-out boards, I wait for him and catch my breath.

Then the doubts sneak in. What was I thinking? He's been tied up for who knows how long and he's injured. I left him there alone to face two guys with guns. Some rescuer I am. We should've stuck together. Things are always better when we're together. He should've been here by now. Where is he? Should I go back?

Oh, dear God. Please keep him safe.

Chapter 19

Jake

I can't believe Sophie actually showed up. There she was in the shadows, an answer to prayer. *Thanks, God.* What an idiot I am for shutting her out in the first place. I send her back through the tunnel so I can keep her safe while the circulation comes back to my legs. As I watch her head back down the tunnel I realize I better not lose focus now. This nightmare isn't over yet.

Before I'm totally recovered, Tony reenters. He's briefly blinded as he comes in from the bright sunlight glistening off the snow. I wait to make my move, trying to ignore the pinprickly feeling in my legs.

"I looked all around; didn't see anything but some firecrackers. Someone was here. Bowers better hurry. We've got to get out of here soon."

Firecrackers? How'd she manage that?

His eyes finally adjust as the blood starts to move to my extremities. He stares confused as Grady starts to sit up, rubbing his jaw. They both glare at me. I hope Sophie made it down.

"Take him out, now!" screams the deputy.

Tony points his gun as Grady searches for his weapon. My cue to leave. I turn and stumble into the shadows, my legs not fully cooperating yet. Grabbing my backpack, I scramble back down the tunnel. A gunshot reverberates through the enclosed area.

I limp along as fast as I can but hear them coming quickly behind me. Don't panic, Taylor, you have the advantage. You know this tunnel and they don't. Yeah, but I hadn't counted on bullets whizzing past my head when I visualized my escape. *Okay, Lord, please keep taking care of Sophie and me.* The darkness of the tunnel slows their pursuit. I pull out the small flashlight from my backpack to help guide my way. I hear them cursing and yelling and soon notice a larger flashlight beam bounce around the walls.

As I run, I pull my skateboard out of my backpack. When I had been studying the map of the mine, I noticed there was a mining cart track running through the tunnel.

It reminded me of the rails at the skate park where I spent hours mastering my tricks. I brought the skateboard along in case there was any chance of riding them. As I hit the steep slope of the tunnel, I drop the board on the rails and fly down. Memorizing the details of the mine pays off. I know when to crouch and jump, catching air and flying over the twisted metal of the broken track. I land, then grab my board and start to run.

The men, however, stumble down the hill, swearing and banging into carts and old equipment. The screams of pain that echo through the mine make me cringe. I'm pretty sure at least one of them has met up with that broken track. More shots are fired, and my adrenaline shoots up. The blasts cause the tunnel to shake and dirt falls from the ceiling. *Please, God, don't let this place collapse.*

The faint green of the glow stick guides my way. I reach for it as I pass, then remember what Sophie said about wanting them to follow us, so I leave it in place. Dodging around the barrels and tools, I make my way toward the library. More crashes behind me tell me my pursuers are not far behind.

As I approach the heavy wooden beam doorway, someone jumps out at me.

"Jake!" It's Sophie.

I grab her hand and together we sprint as fast as possible down the corridor, up the stairs, and into the room behind the library. We burst through the secret passageway, stumbling and sliding across the library floor as a startled Sheriff Miller whips out his gun and aims it at us. I stare at the barrel of the gun and point back at the library wall. Sophie clings to me.

Sheriff Miller swings around with his gun cocked as Deputy Grady bursts through with his weapon drawn. The two men stare at each other, both looking disoriented and bewildered.

I'm thrilled to see Sheriff Miller. Sophie somehow must have convinced him to come. But as he looks at us sprawled out on the floor, he does not appear happy to see us. He keeps his gun drawn, his eyes darting back and forth between Deputy Grady and us. Obviously he has no idea what's going on. Instinctively, I put my arm around Sophie.

"What's going on?!" Sheriff Miller shouts.

"I tried to tell you Deputy Grady was up to no good. He's the one who slashed my tires and planted the joint in my jeep," I blurt out, trying to explain.

Deputy Grady quickly gathers his wits and lowers his gun.

"Not this again. Ben, I thought someone broke in here and came to check out the situation. I didn't know it was only the love birds sneaking away together," says the deputy.

"I got a call a little while ago that the library had been broken into. The window of the back door has been smashed in," says the sheriff.

"Well, I guess we found the culprits. Case solved," Deputy Grady responds.

"I thought you were out of town, Lee," Sheriff Miller says to him, not lowering his weapon.

"I just got back," says the lying piece of garbage.

"Sheriff Miller, please listen," I interrupt as Sophie and I get to our feet. I keep my arm around her; she's shaking. "He's up to no good. And I found proof."

The sheriff looks at Sophie. Still stunned, she just nods.

"What proof?"

"It's in the mine. There are crates full of cocaine up at the entrance. Deputy Grady and his buddies have been storing it there, then sending it to the resort towns."

Sheriff Miller looks from me to his deputy.

"You have to believe me. They're planning on moving the supply today." I've got to convince him.

"Ben, the kid is crazy," Deputy Grady says.

"Sheriff Miller." Sophie finally stops trembling enough to speak. "It's true. I saw it. They've been holding Jake hostage up there. I was the one who broke the back window this morning and called you to get you to come here."

"I know it sounds crazy, but let us show you," I add. "There's an injured man in the tunnels. I think he may need some medical assistance."

Sheriff Miller continues to look between all of us, contemplating who to believe.

"Let's all take a walk together and check it out," he finally says.

Deputy Grady's poker face starts to crack as his shifty eyes go from the front door to the hidden passageway.

Sheriff Miller takes notice. "Lee, is there a problem?"

Deputy Grady slowly raises his gun back up.

"Yeah, I'm not going back in there."

"Lee?" A look of disbelief washes over Sheriff Miller's face.

"I'm not going down for this."

"Is all that true? Are you really a part of the drug ring we've been trying to catch?"

We watch the stare-down between the mentor and his trusted apprentice. Just like a standoff from those old westerns Dad and I used to watch—the good sheriff verses the evil crook, with guns drawn and eyes locked. Who will back down?

Deputy Grady finally breaks the silence. "I'm walking out of here. And you're going to let me."

"Sorry, son, but you know I can't do that," answers Sheriff Miller and pulls the trigger, shooting the gun right out of the deputy's hand.

Sophie screams at the explosive blast. As she buries her face in my chest, I pull her close protectively.

The startled deputy grabs his wrist then slowly raises his hands. In one swift move, Sheriff Miller whips Grady's arm behind his back, slapping on the handcuffs. Glad to see the old sheriff has quick reflexes. After he secures Deputy Grady to the metal stair railing and reads him his rights, Sheriff Miller radios for an ambulance. Then he follows us back through the secret passageway. Sophie grabs my hand. As we enter the tunnels we can hear Tony's screams.

While we hurry toward what sounds like a wounded animal, I finish telling the sheriff about the drug operation at the mine.

"The crates are filled with bags of white powder at the mine entrance. They got nervous when I stumbled onto their set-up, that's why they slashed my tires and planted the marijuana. They're planning on moving the stash today. Two others are coming with a truck. The guy in charge is named Bowers."

"I can't believe this has been going on right under my nose."

Using my flashlight, I lead Sheriff Miller through the tunnel toward the dull green glow. Sophie stays back, not wanting to see the carnage. Can't blame her. Poor Tony has impaled his leg on the broken track. Blood oozes out as he screams in agony. Sheriff Miller takes off his belt to use as a tourniquet, then orders me to take Sophie back to the library.

"Wait there for me." He does not sound happy with us. So much for being heroes.

As we walk back, I glance at my phone and see all the missed calls and texts from my parents, Rachel, Tommy, Chad, and Sophie. I guess there is one category I've missed in my analysis of people. Not only are there Walkers, Talkers, and Stalkers, but there are actually those who truly care about me. I close my eyes and send a quick thank-you to God for keeping us safe and allowing the truth to be revealed. I promise him I won't forget what he's done for me. Then I turn to Sophie.

"Sophie, I don't know how to thank you."

"I'm just glad you're alright."

"You saved me. When I was up there, not sure I'd make it out alive, I remembered everything you said and started to pray. God answered my prayer by sending you."

She blushes.

"I can't believe you found me. I was afraid you didn't get my text."

"It took me awhile to figure it out, once I finally looked at it. I was so mad at you I may never have read it if it wasn't for your mom."

"I know you think I blindsided you, but the only reason I told you I didn't want to see you anymore was to keep you safe. There was no bet with Chad."

"That's what Chad said, but I didn't really believe him."

"I was the one blindsided. By my own success. I know I've been a jerk, but that's not who I am. Sophie, you're the best thing that's happened to me since I moved here. Will you give me another chance?"

"What did you have in mind?" she asks cautiously.

"How about I take you to the Snow Ball tonight?"

"What?"

"The Snow Ball—I assume it's tonight."

"Yes, but you've had your face bashed in, been fired at, tied up for a day, and your hand looks so bad after fighting with the deputy I think the hospital should be your next stop. Why on earth would you want to go to the dance?"

"Why? As much fun as a hospital sounds, I'd much rather spend the evening dancing with an amazing, smart, funny, interesting, beautiful girl who has the most incredible green eyes I've ever seen. Sophie, will you go to the dance with me?"

"Hmm . . . only if you can do a leading man move," she says with a sly smile.

"You mean a chick flick leading man move."

"Of course. Sometimes the tough guy needs to show his softer side."

"I'll try my best, my lady," I answer with a bow.

Chapter 20

Sophie

"Sophie, that was a stupid risk you took today," my dad lectures on the drive home, as if we hadn't gone over all this a million times already. The last few hours were a whirlwind as the library swarmed with law enforcement, EMTs who tended to Jake's injuries, and, of course, our stunned parents. Deputy Grady admitted to sabotaging Jake's jeep, planting the marijuana, and leaking the story to the press. Bowers and another guy were apprehended at the top of the mine trying to move the crates of drugs. The injured guy in the tunnel was arrested and taken to the hospital.

"What time is it?" Dad's lecture is totally cutting into my getting-ready-for-the-dance time.

"What? Why?"

"The dance." Duh.

"Forget the dance, you were almost killed today!" Dad won't let it drop.

"But I'm Okay. You should be proud of me for helping to stop the drug ring."

"I still don't understand why you didn't ask for help," Mom says.

"Would you have believed me if I said, 'Hey, Mom and Dad, Jake sent me a secret message that I think means he's being held hostage up in the mine by Deputy Grady'?"

My parents exchange a look, proving my point.

"But this isn't like you to do something so . . ." Dad says, searching for the right word.

"Adventurous?" I ask.

"Reckless," he says. "I wish Jake hadn't involved you."

"He tried to keep me out of it. That's why he told me he didn't want to see me anymore. But then he needed my help."

"Thank goodness neither of you were seriously hurt," Mom says.

"I should have known something was up sooner. I've gotten to know him better over the last few weeks. He doesn't necessarily advertise it, but he's a good guy. He just wouldn't do drugs or use me."

"He's lucky you believed him," my mom adds as we pull into the driveway. "But don't think this is over. Your dad's right—what you did was dangerous. There will be some consequences, once we figure out what they are."

"Okay." As long as they don't interfere with tonight, who cares? "By the way, I won't need a ride to the dance tonight," I holler as I run into the house.

Taking the stairs two at a time I move as fast as I can. Every possible second is needed to pull off this makeover. I jump in the shower and try to get all the dirt out of my hair. I only have an hour till the dance begins. How will I ever get ready? My panic over the time keeps my nerves about my date with Jake in check, though.

I blow-dry my hair, trying to figure out what to do with it, when a soft knock on the door interrupts my big decision.

"Come in."

"Hi, sweetheart," my mom says as she enters. "I still can't believe everything you and Jake have been through today. When I think how things could have turned out, my hands start to shake."

"I didn't mean to scare you but I had to help him. Poor Mrs. Taylor. Do you think she's stopped crying yet?"

"She's been through a lot the last few days. Are you sure going to the dance is a good idea? It's hard to let you go out tonight and not keep you home safe with us. I'm sure the Taylors feel the same way."

"Mom, the whole town will be at the dance. You can all keep an eye on us there."

"Don't think we won't. You know, I hate to say I told you so, but I knew Jake liked you," she teases.

"Yeah, I guess he does. I still can't believe it though. I mean, he's totally amazing."

"He's the lucky one."

She helps me curl my hair while I paint my nails, then she leaves me to mess with my make-up and get dressed.

My parents stand at the bottom of the stairs as I descend. I know I look pretty good, but their expressions take me by surprise. Mom beams and Dad's eyes fill with tears.

"Sophie, you look stunning," Dad quietly says when I reach the bottom step.

He hugs me and helps me on with my wrap, then ushers me to the front door. When he opens it, the sight in front of me takes my breath away.

Parked in front of my house is a sleigh. Two elegant white horses stand regally at the front, sparkling white lights trim the sleigh, and a driver with a top hat smiles at me. Standing beside the sleigh, holding a single red rose in his hand and looking exquisitely handsome in a slim charcoal grey suit, is Jake. It is the most beautiful sight I've ever seen.

Dad takes my arm and leads me down the porch steps. Jake meets us at the bottom and holds out the rose.

"Sophie, you look gorgeous," Jake says.

"You look pretty spectacular yourself."

While Jake and my dad shake hands, they have a brief exchange.

"Straight to the dance. No adventures tonight."

"Yes, Dr. Metcalf."

Jake offers me his arm and leads me to the sleigh. He helps me up, then walks around to the other side and climbs in. As he places a blanket over our laps, the driver leads the horses down my street. I glance back at my parents, who are busy taking photos of us.

"Well," Jake says, "how'd I do?"

"Wow. How did you have time to set this up?"

"Mitchell's dad runs sleigh rides this time of year."

"Hi, Mr. Moore," I call.

He tips his hat in response.

"Is there anything you can't do?"

"Rescue myself."

"Did you mean what you said earlier? That I was the best thing that has happened to you since you moved here?" I ask shyly.

"Sitting up there, not sure if I'd ever get out alive, made me think about things. I realized you were right. I've been a jerk for the past six months, enamored by the fame. But I know now that everything I have can be gone in an instant. I can't take any of it for granted and I need to focus on what's truly important."

Thank you, God, for this incredible day.

As we ride through the winter wonderland with the stars twinkling overhead, I think about the last few days. I may never experience the thrill of the halfpipe, but after all I've been through—from the excitement of taking off on a new romance, the twists and turns of devastation when Jake dumped me, terror from all that happened in the mine, and stunned realization that he actually cares for me—I may have a sense of what it would feel like.

I look up at Jake and smile. He smiles back, then he slowly leans in, gently touches my cheek, and kisses me. When his lips touch mine, my heart soars and then flutters with pure bliss. That must be how it feels to land the perfect blindside.

❄

Once the news broke about how Jake and I uncovered and brought down a dangerous drug smuggling operation, our quiet little town once again was media mayhem. Jake went from Olympic Superstar to National Hero.

The interviews and magazine covers started anew. Usually, my part in the adventure was overlooked, but I didn't mind. I realized I was more comfortable on the sidelines where I was busy writing the story, from all angles. If that doesn't get the colleges' attention, nothing will.

Jake Taylor really is amazing. He now realizes the influence he has and is trying hard to be a good role model to all his fans. Also, he and his parents have begun attending our church. Father Scott has even encouraged him to speak at a few youth conferences about finding ways to use your talents and interests to glorify God.

Jake still travels a lot for training, competitions, interviews, and as many Special Olympic events as he can go to. But he always comes back to Silver Springs and to me. I can't wait for our next adventure to begin.

Leslea Wahl

lives in beautiful Colorado
with her husband and three
children. Their own life of
adventure includes traveling,
skiing, and scuba diving.
Leslea strives to write fiction
that will inspire readers to
use their own talents and
gifts to glorify God.
Visit Leslea's website at
www.LesleaWahl.com.

 **TEEN** promises you stories that:

reflect your life experience

deal with tough topics

take your questions seriously

have a sense of humor

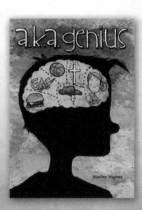

don't talk at you, over you,
or down to you

explore living your faith in
the real world

Our teen books accept
who you are here and
now and inspire you to
recognize who God
calls you to become.

Pauline TEEN

Who: The Daughters of St. Paul

What: Pauline Teen—linking your life to Jesus Christ and his Church

When: 24/7

Where: All over the world and on www.pauline.org

Why: Because our life-long passion is to witness to God's amazing love for all people!

How: Inspiring lives of holiness through: Apps, digital media, concerts, websites, social media, videos, blogs, books, music albums, radio media literacy, DVDs, ebooks, stores, conferences, bookfairs, parish exhibits, personal contac illustration, vocation talks, pho writing, editing, graphic design marketing, interviews

BOOKS & MEDIA

The Daughters of St. Paul operate book and media centers at the
following addresses. Visit, call, or write the one nearest you today,
or find us at www.pauline.org.

CALIFORNIA
3908 Sepulveda Blvd, Culver City, CA 90230   310-397-8676
935 Brewster Avenue, Redwood City, CA 94063   650-369-4230
5945 Balboa Avenue, San Diego, CA 92111   858-565-9181

FLORIDA
145 SW 107th Avenue, Miami, FL 33174   305-559-6715

HAWAII
1143 Bishop Street, Honolulu, HI 96813   808-521-2731

ILLINOIS
172 North Michigan Avenue, Chicago, IL 60601   312-346-4228

LOUISIANA
4403 Veterans Memorial Blvd, Metairie, LA 70006   504-887-7631

MASSACHUSETTS
885 Providence Hwy, Dedham, MA 02026   781-326-5385

MISSOURI
9804 Watson Road, St. Louis, MO 63126   314-965-3512

NEW YORK
64 West 38th Street, New York, NY 10018   212-754-1110

SOUTH CAROLINA
243 King Street, Charleston, SC 29401   843-577-0175

TEXAS
Currently no book center; for parish exhibits or outreach evangelization,
contact: 210-569-0500 or SanAntonio@paulinemedia.com
or P.O. Box 761416, San Antonio, TX 78245

VIRGINIA
1025 King Street, Alexandria, VA 22314   703-549-3806

CANADA
3022 Dufferin Street, Toronto, ON M6B 3T5   416-781-9131

Smile
God loves you